A Squire's Wish

Book 2 of
The Hidden Wishes Series

A GameLit Novel

by

Tao Wong

Copyright

A Squire's Wish
Copyright © 2018 Tao Wong. All rights reserved.
Copyright © 2018 Sarah Anderson Cover Designer

A Starlit Publishing Book
Published by Starlit Publishing
PO Box 30035
High Park PO
Toronto, ON
M6P 3K0
Canada

www.starlitpublishing.com

Ebook ISBN: 978177538096
Paperback ISBN: 9781989458662

Books in the

Hidden Wishes series

A Gamer's Wish

A Squire's Wish

A Jinn's Wish

Contents

Chapter 1

"This would be a lot easier if I was allowed to use magic." I exhaled audibly and twisted my shoulders, my arms throbbing. Still, at least we were finally inside our new duplex. Three bedrooms, two bathrooms, hardwood floors, and a living room meant I was paying much more than I wanted. But, considering Alexa had insisted on the larger space, and she was paying half, I'd compromised. I had to admit, looking around the relatively modern, open-plan space, it looked nice. Even if all the belongings I had from my bachelor suite barely filled our new home.

"Oh please, this is barely a workout," Alexa said as she impatiently tapped her foot. The Nordic blonde was more Wonder Woman than model and had more muscles in her arms than I did, so it was no surprise she was barely out of breath.

"Mage," I said and pointed to myself as I struggled to catch my breath. Though perhaps I could do with a little more actual exercise.

"The enforcers in the Mage Council are as well known for their physical prowess as they are for their magical abilities," Alexa said. I grunted, refusing to acknowledge her point, even while being intrigued by the idea of buff magic users. I guessed real-world magicians were more like anime heroes than Raistlin. In either case, the initiate was more likely to know than I did. The Templars had been the church's sharp edge against the supernatural world for hundreds of years. They'd been occasional allies and enemies of the Mage Council throughout the years. Me? I'd barely entered the supernatural world six months ago. I still had a lot to catch up on.

"Fine. So I might be slacking off on the entire exercise bit," I muttered as I bent my knees to grab the edge of the couch once again.

"Slacking off implies you ever started," Lily said behind me, her arms full with a cardboard box helpfully labeled "books." The olive-skinned, slim and shapely jinn sauntered toward us from the front door where we'd deposited our initial run with a sway of her hips. "Where do you want these?"

"What are they?" I grunted out as we maneuvered the couch to catch the sunlight and to face where we'd decided the TV would go.

"Reference material."

"Huh?" I said as I squatted and set my end of the couch on the floor.

"Your role-playing books." The jinn held the heavy box of books with one hand as she scratched her nose, obviously not bothered with things like weight. No surprise there. Her "body" wasn't really real, just a magical construct, which begged the question why I was doing the heavy lifting, but that would open up a whole different can of worms regarding Lily's increasing agoraphobia.

"Right. We'll keep those in the living room," I said and pointed to the corner we'd designated for the bookcases. For a moment, I felt amazed as the reality of my situation hit me once again. Not the shacking up with two stunning, supermodel-level, good-looking women but the fact that I was a mage—a mage wielding magic through a wish granted by a jinn who based my entire leveling progression off a homebrew mixture of role-playing game books, single-player video games, and massive multiplayer online games. It was how my old RPG books became reference material.

"Stop delaying. We've only got the moving van till five," Alexa said, urging me out the front door.

"You sure I can't do this with magic?"

"After you left the dent in the doorway of our old apartment?" Alexa said derisively. "We can't afford to pay to fix another mistake."

"Fine." I grumbled as we reached the moving van and went for the bed stand. Alexa was not wrong. We still needed to find the money for mattresses and bed frames for both girls. Or technically, for me since I'd given my bed to Alexa. "Let's get this over with."

***

Hours later, the three of us were seated in our new living room, evening sunlight streaming in from the blinds as we preyed on four large pizzas. I shook my head, amazed once again at the sheer volume of food both women managed to put away. Admittedly, today I was putting on a good showing. Not that it was a competition.

"So, Caleb gave you today off? Alexa asked.

"Yes. After I threatened to continue using 'What Does the Fox Say?' as my training tune for Gong," I said with a grin. Since Lily basically downloaded spells into my brain at each level increase, my understanding of actual magical theory was, shall we say, erratic. It didn't help that much of the magic theory she downloaded came from millennia of magical knowledge—knowledge gained as the assistant or tool of world-class magicians. While I might have more powerful spells than my more traditionally trained counterparts, mine were also more esoteric and not as easily pliable with modern magical theory. To fix my magical shortcomings, Caleb, the master mage sent to deal with me from the Mage Council, had set up a training program. One aspect of which was teaching me to understand and manipulate the components of the spells I had in my brain.

In the case of Gong, the spell manipulated sound waves via magic. Like most spells, Gong, for all its outward simplicity, was significantly more complex internally than its final manifestation. To channel the spell, I had to control the amount of mana input, where the mana went to adjust volume and pitch, as well as dictate the location the noise would appear. All this was controlled by strings of arcane glyphs and, in some cases, actual mathematical formulas. Combined, they were known as spell formulas. Right now, my training involved learning to repeatedly cast the spell with specific target notes. I had to play a song with my spell.

Technically, I was doing this in the least mana efficient manner possible. There were actual spells that allowed its user to continually channel the spell, formulating the song in one continual cast. The problem was the spell formula for such a song was significantly more complex than the simple spell Lily had downloaded into my mind. It was kind of like the difference between playing "Chopsticks" and Mozart. When I'd asked, Caleb had displayed the simplest musical spell formula he knew for me to read just to shut me up. The formula itself was intriguing, a mixture of—

"Earth to Henry," Lily said, waving a hand in front of my eyes.

"Sorry," I said, pushing her hand away. "Was just thinking of a spell."

"Of course you were," Lily said with a snort. "Maybe you should be thinking about a quest instead. If you haven't forgotten, you're broke."

"We're broke," I said pointedly. "I still don't get why you need a room of your own. You have your ring."

"Which I've lived in for hundreds of years," Lily said, glaring at me. "You try going back to your cell. Even if the door's open—"

"Ah, right," I said and scratched my head. Sometimes I forgot Lily was basically a slave to the ring since she never actually lived in it anymore. While she had twisted my first wish to give her a way to stay out of the ring itself, past users hadn't been as careless or generous. "Sorry."

"It's fine," Lily said with a wave of her hand.

"I do not understand, however, why you cannot form your own furnishings," Alexa asked Lily.

"If you recall, I'm bound by the rules of the ring. I can't really affect the outside world in a meaningful manner with my magic without a wish," Lily said with a little bite. I guess some insults, like the Templars trying to kill me and steal my ring via Alexa, were not so easily forgiven.

"Wait. With your magic?" I said. "I thought you couldn't do it period."

"Well…" Lily paused, looking embarrassed. "It's a bit complicated."

"Complicated… like you-don't-want-to-get-a-job complicated?" I said threateningly. While I'd been scrambling to earn an income by completing requests and other small jobs in the magical community, Lily had stayed home playing computer games… and begging me to get a console.

"Well, I'm not exactly legal, am I?" Lily asked. "I don't have any proof of identification. You wouldn't want me to be deported or thrown into jail, would you?"

"That…" I paused to consider as I looked at Lily. Well, yes. She was a Middle Eastern woman in the country. Technically illegally. Then again, she was a jinn who could literally disappear with a thought, which would make for a really interesting police report. But… "Thousand hells."

"Right," Lily said with a smile when she won her point. "That's why it's better I stay back home. Also, the more games I play, the better the patches I can provide."

Once again, I noted how she also avoided mentioning her growing reluctance to even visit the outside world. I considered bringing it up and once again shied away from the topic. Tackling sensitive emotional issues headlong was not something my traditional Chinese household had readied me for.

"Please don't." Alexa interrupted my thoughts with her words. "Your last patch had him sitting at the beach picking up rocks for an hour, muttering about leveling up his 'analyze' skill."

"Hey, it's a staple cheat skill," Lily said.

"Not the way you implemented it," I said. It was only after I had spent some time talking to Lily that I realized the only way to upgrade the analyze skill while staring at rocks would have been to read books on geology first, then spend the time actually perusing the rocks. And then repeating the task over and over again.

"Everyone's a critic," Lily said and crossed her arms to glare at us.

"As the lab rat, yes I am," I said. "Let's just focus on magic, okay?"

"Speaking of that, what are your… stats?" Alexa said, almost too casually. Really, the knight initiate sucked at casual. It just wasn't something they taught at knight school. It didn't help that I knew she was asking because the Templars, like most of the other major powers in the know, were waiting for me to hit level one hundred. Once I did, the ring could finally come off my fingers without it being lost forever.

Still, she was my closest ally. And I had no reason not to show her since Caleb received almost daily updates.

Class: Mage
Level 21 (19% Experience)
Known Spells: Light Sphere, Force Spear, Force Shield, Force Fingers, Alter Temperature, Gong, Gust, Heal, Healing Ward, Link, Track, Fix, Ward, Glamour, Illusion, Summon, Iceball, Fireball

Magical Skillset
Mana Flow: 4/10
Mana to Energy Conversion: 3/10
Spell Container: 3/10
Spatial Location: 3/10
Spatial Movement: 3/10
Energy Manipulation: 4/10
Biological Manipulation: 3/10
Matter Manipulation: 1/10
Summoning: 1/10
Duration: 4/10

14

"You gained two levels," Alexa said in approval. "But only learned one new spell?"

"Blame Caleb," I said, disgruntled. "He convinced Lily I needed to spend more time understanding my current repertoire. He wants her to stop giving me spells entirely."

"That," Alexa said and then fell silent, compressing her lips together tightly on the sentence she had been about to utter.

"Sucks. I know." I sighed. Truth be told, I somewhat agreed with Caleb's reasoning. I'd gained so many spells, I often did not use most of them. For quite a few, I had synchronicity of less than 50 percent when I cast them, never mind linking them together. No, for a while, I needed to work on my fundamentals. If I could increase my basic magical skill set to five, I'd be considered an actual novice mage by the Council, someone who at least was worth some basic respect. Of course, the fact this was a logarithmic progression meant that once I got there, the next steps were going to be incrementally harder.

"So. Quests," Lily said leadingly, pushing forth a sheaf of papers. I groaned, staring at the quests—work orders, really—but picked them up. We needed the money.

Chapter 2

The first time I ever saw a four-hundred-pound orc charge down a football field in spiked shoulder pads and a helmet, it was an impressive and bed-wetting sight. The second time, I might've frozen in fear, wondering if I'd written my will. By the third quarter, it was routine.

"And why did we have to be here now?" I muttered, shifting on the too-hard seat. Who willingly spent their evenings unpaid, sitting on hard, metal benches—which were open to the elements—and screaming their head off at the sight of one team pummeling the other? At least when I was gaming, I did it in a temperature-controlled room with cheap, store-bought snacks on hand. "The contract's for after the game is done."

"Are you not enjoying the sight of martial excellence?" Alexa asked as the lines reset. On one side, a full team of orcs stood with control of the ball, each of them fully dressed and padded. On the other, a smaller—literally—team of dwarves stood across the field, ready to defend their turf.

"Not at all. I'm just hoping we didn't undercharge them," I said, eying the field over the cover of my book. When I had pulled it out, I received more than a few glares, but those subsided when they realized it was a spellbook. Being a mage still commanded some respect, thankfully. If not more comfortable seats.

The field itself was a torn and bloody mess, the grass and earth looking like it had been tiled by a rototiller with a grudge. Particular portions showcased the extra-violent nature of the sport, blood and guts mashed into the ground. And all over the field, I could see the light glow of mana as the illusion array ensured the mundanes were kept in the dark.

"Come on, it's not that hard. Is it?" Alexa dropped her voice to a whisper at the end, and her eyes shone with concern. Our job—my job—was to clean up the mess after the match was over. After losing their resident contracted dryad, the Supernatural Football League of Erie had contacted us. If we managed to do a good job, we'd actually have a regular contract, at least when the season was on. It'd be a nice change of pace from our regular scramble for jobs.

"Don't know," I said to Alexa just as softly. "I've never tried to manipulate this much earth and grass. Theoretically, linking multiple Healing Wards together with some direct manipulation on my part should speed up the growth of the grass. All I need to do beforehand is tamp down the earth and smooth it out, which an adjusted Force Spear should do well enough. It'd be more like a Force Plow, but it should work."

"Good." Alexa turned back to watching the orcs and dwarfs beat the shit out of each other under the guise of sport. I sighed slightly and watched the initiate for a second, seeing how she leaned forward, lips parted and eyes glinting with interest and enjoyment. Jocks. I would never understand them.

***

I frowned, adjusting the position of the warding block once again. After finally being happy with it, I moved down another twenty feet to set up the next block. Each of these warding blocks had been hand carved by me, their glyphs and spell formulas painstakingly cast beforehand. Along the field, Alexa walked back and forth, spreading fertilizer across the churned earth.

"How much longer is this going to take?" grumbled the large red-skinned, horned demon— Japanese demon that was, an oni. "Edith never took so long."

"Edith was an eighty-year-old dryad linked to the very earth itself, who had been doing this job for forty years," I replied as I pulled another block out. "And if you had confirmed the contract yesterday like we mentioned, I could have set up and buried these wards beforehand. Now, I've got to do the prep."

"This better work. For the amount we're paying you—"

"Which is two-thirds what you paid Edith," I said, staring at him. "Don't think I don't know it. But we let you do so because we aren't as good as she is."

"Whatever. Just get it done right," Ken said and walked off. I glared after the demon, my sight defocusing for a moment to see the fat, coverall-wearing figure he showed the outside world. Somehow, I felt the glamour was much more fitting for the caustic ass.

Left alone, I worked my way around the field and finally set all the blocks in place. I'd have loved to plant them deep, and perhaps I might another time, but until we confirmed the contract, I was not going to lose my warding blocks. Even if they were cheap hand-carved wooden blocks, they still took a decent amount of time to create. And if I ever wanted to increase their power, I would need to start working with some better materials. That being said, wood itself was a great material for my next spell.

Finally done, I took the next step, using a Force Plow to smooth the earth. Really, it was just a Force Spear with its container adjusted. It had taken just over three hours to work out how to create the Force Plow, adjusting the formula for the container so the spell formed the necessary shape and, more importantly, held together. Still, this was the first time I was using it for such a duration, so the worms in my stomach refused to stop shifting.

Stupid really. No one was going to die here. I'd just lose a little contract. But part of the reason I had stayed as low key—or a drudge, as my sister named me years ago—was that I hated pressure. I hated to make mistakes and lose face.

"Henry?" Alexa called after I'd been standing still for a few minutes.

"Just checking the spell over," I replied, using a lame excuse. Raising my hand, I started the casting motions required, fingers flicking, twitching, and spreading as I cast. The physical motions were technically unnecessary, as were the words I softly chanted. Magic itself was all about intention and magical formulas, with the formulas more a mental guide than necessity. But the motions and words helped. The spell slid into a universal groove, which helped reduce the cost and difficulty of casting my spell. When formed, the Force Plow was invisible for the most part. To my eyes, it consisted of three portions. The first was a slightly blunted blade that helped level the earth, with excess dirt collected in the second, covered portion. The extra dirt was then compressed into the earth by a rolling cylinder of force.

"Huh. Never seen anyone do that," Ken exclaimed, grudging admiration in his voice.

I glowed slightly at his words, though I didn't tell Ken the truth. The spell might look impressive, but it only worked because, relatively speaking, the amount of damage done to the grounds wasn't that great. I was only shifting around a foot of earth at most at each location. My spell and mana were nowhere near sufficient enough to say, compress asphalt. Yet.

Thirty minutes later, the ground was as smooth as I could make it. I paused, panting, and eyed the glowing blue line from the corner of my eyes. With a wave to Alexa, who walked the grounds again with more fertilizer, I slumped and waited for my mana to regenerate.

A part of me pointed out I should be attempting to meditate. Well, not exactly meditate. That's the wrong word, even if Caleb does use it. Cultivate? That makes it sound like I'm some Eastern immortal. "Open myself to the world" sounds too hippy-like. Whatever the case, it was a process to expand the refresh rate of my mana, of opening myself to the world's energy to draw it in. I didn't of course. Among other things, I sucked at the skill itself, and I looked like a complete fool doing it.

"Why are you stopping?" Ken asked, stomping back toward me and leaving fresh boot prints in my smooth earth.

"Two reasons. I need more mana for the next part. And we need to make sure there's enough fertilizer."

"Edith—"

"Was a dryad. She could draw nutrients from the surroundings and pour mana directly into the plants to nourish them. I can't," I said. Of course, I knew that theoretically there was a way to do so, but considering my mana pool and my lack of understanding of biological processes, I was so not going to. Healing—or in my case, accelerated growth—was already risky. Luckily, grass didn't care about cancer.

Ken rolled his big, bulbous red eyes at me again before stomping away. Once again, I took the time to check over the wards and then began the slow process of linking them together in my spell. It was not particularly difficult, just complex, casting Link and holding each Link spell in place as I cast and added another to the chain. Each one led back to me and the tuft of grass I held in my hand, forming a giant spell rectangle bordered by my wards.

When I finally cast my Heal spell, it would trigger the grass to grow, replicating and covering the churned earth with freshly grown grass. I was particularly proud of the fact that since the spell was Linked and targeted at the grass I held in hand, it wouldn't affect the various weeds, earthworms, and bugs living in the soil. It was both more mana efficient and smarter this way.

"Done," Alexa called to me and I sighed, looking into the sky as I began the last spell process. Such a simple thing, Heal Linked to the grass with wards to denote the boundaries of the spell. Even as my mana dropped, the untouched grass could visibly be seen growing while the newly tamped-down earth slowly began to sprout. I found myself swaying slightly, the spell draining more mana than I had anticipated, the loss making my face grow pale.

Linked Heal (Modified) Cast
Synchronicity 87%

"Henry," Alexa called to me as she neared, seeing my predicament.

I shook my head, knowing that if I gave up now, the spell would collapse on itself. While not dangerous—except to me—I wasn't exactly sure I could pull it off again, not with the pounding headache I'd already gained. Better to complete the job. And it was working. Already, I could see blades of grass poking out of the earth, slowly growing lusher.

"Damn it, Henry." Alexa stomped toward me and kicked my shin. The sudden pain broke my concentration, the spell unravelling. The backlash of the broken spell made me cry out and clutch at my head. "Lily warned you not to overexert yourself."

As I sat, cradling my head and eyeing the deep-red flashing mana bar, I growled at Alexa. Damn woman wore steel-toed boots. I was going to have a very big bruise there tomorrow. Yet, as my head cleared a little, I stared around the now-green fields with more than a little pride.

Magic was beautiful, complex, and amazing. Even after so many months training and learning, I still found myself marveling at the fact that I could wield such power. I could bring life to a trampled field and, perhaps most importantly, get paid.

Chapter 3

After overexerting myself spending mana, I'd been relegated to book study for the next couple days. It was frustrating, but I understood their concerns. Lily and Caleb had more than once described the dangers of mana withdrawal and overexertion. Increasing your mana pool required work, just like building muscles. The more you did and the closer you were to your limit, the more you built. However, do too much or too fast, and you created instabilities in your body. Ligaments and tendons took longer to develop in the human body than muscle mass. Mana channels and networks took longer to widen and strengthen than a body's central mana pool. My levels were, in many cases, Lily directly intervening and increasing my mana pool, but it would take a while for my body to catch up, even bolstered by her magics. Even the jinn feared directly manipulating a human body too greatly. The risks of cancer, tumors, and other unwanted mutations were not to be taken lightly.

And so here I was, lounging in my chair, working my way through another damn book. The door swung open, and Alexa walked in with a slouch from her training session. I frowned, staring at the blonde Amazon as she threw her sports bag full of workout gear, her spear, and toy weapons aside before she stomped up the stairs toward her room.

"What was that about?" I muttered.

Lily ignored my words, either because she had not heard or was refusing to hear. Our relative silence was punctuated a short while later by the slamming of a door and further large, obvious stomping. Minutes later, a door opened and then another slammed shut before the sound of water running through old pipes made its way to us.

Blessed silence ensued for all of fifteen minutes before the sound of loud stomping feet reappeared, and Alexa descended the stairs. Her short hair still slightly damp, the initiate threw herself onto the couch, forcing me to scramble quickly to pull my feet aside before they were squished. Once she was down, she sighed loudly.

"Alexa?" I asked softly. "What's wrong?"

"Nothing."

"I see," I said softly, staring at the blonde. I could push the matter, but I decided against it and instead shifted to a more comfortable position and propped my book open.

A few minutes later, a loud sigh broke the silence again.

"You know, if you have something to say, you could just say it." Yeesh. It wasn't as if I had never experienced teenage-girl syndrome, even though Alexa should have been old enough to have gotten over that period. I had to admit, it was amusing to think I was actually finding my sister's teenage youth a blessing.

"Nothing," Alexa snapped back at me before she sighed again.

I rolled my eyes and focused on my book, the silence lingering for a few minutes before it was broken by Alexa.

"I might need to leave."

"Oh?" I frowned, turning my head to the side. Considering Alexa was here because she was "fated" to be, I found her sudden decision interesting. Not that I truly believed in their oracles, but then again, I was a mage. What did I know?

"I'm getting my squire's test," Alexa said.

"Pardon?" I frowned again. "I thought you were going to be a faith healer?"

"So did I, but they feel that because of my 'involvement' with you, I should be a squire," Alexa said bitterly.

"But your healing—"

"Will become a secondary function," Alexa said, "until the jinn situation is resolved." Alexa shot a look at Lily, the jinn completely ignoring the discussion. "And maybe not then."

"Oh. I'm sorry about that," I said softly, grimacing at the fact that somehow my decisions had changed her life. Unintended consequences, they always seemed to play out no matter what I chose.

"*No es nada*," Alexa said with another sigh. "I just need to accept the will of heaven."

I paused, considering her words and then raised a hand slightly to ask the question that had been bugging me. "Is it heaven or the Templars?

Because you being here is your heaven's, but making you a squire seems to be theirs."

"Our heaven," Alexa said, correcting me before she sighed. "In my case, it's the same. Or so says Templar Ignis."

I grunted, shaking my head. I would admit, the idea that anyone, especially someone I might not agree with, could have such control over my life was anathema to me. Then again, I was the guy who refused to get a proper job forever, even when my family and friends had pressured me to do so, just because I hated working for others. The number of jobs I'd been fired from before I learned my lesson was staggering. I sometimes wondered if my reason for doing so was due to my traditionally minded parents. Their views on what was "right," the pressure they exerted on me to "fit," was significant, especially while growing up. Or at least, fit in the doctor, lawyer, accountant, or engineer aspirations they had.

"When are you leaving?" I asked.

"Not sure," Alexa replied with another sigh, eyes half-closing. "Most squires receive a trial or series of trials they must pass to qualify. They're often very similar. We used to joke they'd reach into different helmets to pull out what monster and how many to kill."

"But?"

"But I'm not getting the regular," Alexa said softly. "I'm not allowed. I'm important."

"Oooh." I hissed at her words. I knew that song. The "special treatment" you got when you were unique, potentially better than anyone else. As if somehow, getting something harder and more difficult than what everyone else was doing was supposed to be a damn reward. As if the extra homework, the additional classes were "good" for you.

"Well, if there's anything I can do…"

"Thank you, but I don't want to think about it right now. Do we have any quests outstanding? Something that is easy to finish?"

"Mmm…" I paused, considering, and then waved toward the pile of papers which had accumulated in the corner. "Take your pick. Can't do much right now, but I should be okay for some light work tomorrow."

"I just want to hit something," Alexa said softly, a low growl in her voice.

"Right." I winced at her words and hoped there was a suitable quest in the pile. Because otherwise, I knew exactly what would happen. Alexa would decide I'd had enough of my book studying, drag me to the backyard, and force me to do calisthenics. And then afterward, she would make me practice on the punching bag and target pads. All to give her an excuse to use them as well.

I still had bruises on my thighs… and ribs. And that was with her hitting through the bag last time.

***

"Do you know what a large group of crows is called?" I shouted to Alexa the next day, my hand held in front of me as the Force Shield twisted and distorted before me under assault.

Mystic Crow (Level 9)
HP: 28/28

"No," Alexa said as she finished screwing her spear together. Its durable titanium-and-steel construction allowed her to break it down when not in use for easy transportation. Spear locked in place, Alexa stepped forward, the weapon held close to her body and raised toward the sky. "Can you drop your shield partially?"

"Not going to have a choice in a moment," I said with a snarl. Already, my head was ringing as my spell buckled under the repeated assaults. With an initial synchronicity rating of 38 percent, it was probably one of my worse casts in ages. But surprise and speed had factored greatly into my failure. Alexa, seeing my face distort, nodded.

A moment later, the force shield fell, and the crows descended with a vengeance. Over two dozen crows, each of them as large as a raven with glowing red eyes and claws that gleamed with an eldritch sheen, now had free and unfettered access to us. Luckily, they weren't helicopters, so many had to beat their wings and twist as they turned in a desperate attempt to reach us as quickly as possible.

Alexa thrust her spear forward, hand gliding down the end as her weapon was launched to its farthest extent and plunged into one crow's chest. A quick retraction, with a twist of her body as she did so, smashed another crow aside. The injured bird plummeted to the ground, a wing torn. Without pause, her hands shifted on the spear shaft to strike with the blunt end to beat aside another creature.

While Alexa played offense, my fingers snapped and twirled, my mind flowing through spell formulas without missing a beat. It was a simple spell at first—Gust—but I worked to combine it with another spell, Alter Temperature. Together, the pair of spells formed a gust of bitingly cold wind. I poured mana into the spell, the wind blowing perpendicular and above our forms to push the crows away from us, altering their trajectories and chilling their bones.

Gust Cast
Synchronicity 84%

Alter Temperature Cast
Synchronicity 67%

Spell Combination Success 32%

I said chilling because my spell was not powerful enough to freeze them. I swore, the combined spells I had attempted barely doing more than making the crows think it was a nice autumn day. But the gust itself at least sent most of them flying away from us, giving Alexa another shot at reducing their numbers. Most did not mean all, however. One particular bird managed to wing its way toward me, claws tearing at my hastily raised arm. Pain registered as skin parted under razor-sharp claws, skin and cloth doing little to defend me.

My concentration wavered when I was injured, but training with Caleb and Alexa over these months had some effect. I held the spell together, varying the push of mana into it to alter the strength of the breeze it generated. This shifted the crows erratically, forcing them to battle to stay on target while Alexa had her spear flickering through the air, cutting and sweeping at the birds. Soon enough, the ground was littered with injured avian creatures, forcing the pair of us to back off rather than have our feet pecked to death. Occasionally, I'd bat a too-aggressive crow aside— or attempt to—with my trusty backpack.

For a few passes, our strategy worked. Then, a badly timed gust brought a crow that had been about to miss me directly in line with my face. Panicking, I threw a punch, spearing my own hand on its claws but protecting my face. The pain and surprise made my spell fail while the bird's weight tore its body from my arm.

"Alexa!" I snarled as I kicked the grounded crow away. A flash of darkness in the corner of my eye had me throwing myself all the way to the ground to avoid another pair of crows. Alexa barely reacted to my shout, caught in the middle of a swarm of feathers. I snarled as I stood, taking things into my own hands, my trusty backpack already discarded by my feet. My fingers flicked and twisted as I used my left hand, suddenly glad Caleb had insisted I practice with both hands. Even then, the spell formed badly, the ball of flame nearly missing the bird that was a few feet from my face.

Fireball Cast
Synchronicity 43%
11 points of damage done to Mystic Crow

Literally blown off course by the spell, the crow writhed as flames licked at its body, the flash fire having caught a few of its feathers aflame. Another bird winged its way toward me, and my hasty dodge barely brought me out of range while a wing clipped my injured shoulder. As pain filled my body, I spotted a towering oak tree a short distance away.

"Tree!" I shouted to Alexa, taking off in a zigzag rush during the short break. Many crows had banked, attempting to gain altitude and speed.

To give Alexa time, I turned and cast a series of Mana Darts, my left hand working smoother as I manipulated the shorter spell formula. The invisible projectiles slammed into her harassers, giving Alexa a brief moment of respite, which she used to run with me.

Under the more solid defense of the oak tree and with the ability to put our backs to it, we made our stand again, bleeding and battered. We quickly turned to relying on my Mana Darts to harass the creatures and blast them off branches when they landed while Alexa finished the birds. A few bloody and painful minutes later, we stood victorious but injured.

"That. Was. Not. Easy," I complained, stopping at each word to draw a breath. My chest heaved and sweat covered my body, running into open wounds and sending the stinging sensation through overburdened nerves. I whimpered but still focused on searching for any crows that might be late to the party.

"It was supposed to be," Alexa said, poking the last of the corpses. When she turned toward me, her eyes widened. "Your hand!"

"My head," I added and allowed Alexa to grab my arm to prod and push at my hand. I winced as she focused on the injury, a low glow filling her body and sweeping over my arm. Soon, the ache that had begun to press on me began to fade away, and the torn skin, muscles, and tendons fixed themselves under her care. I grinned slightly, grateful for her ability. The movement of my head made me wince as the mana headache returned with a vengeance. Even her healing could not fix that.

Damn, but Caleb was going to give me shit about overextending myself again.

"What a disappointing performance. A squire should have barely broken a sweat over such a simple request." The voice berating us came from a goateed, muscular man in a simple outdoor jacket and jeans ensemble. If not for the glowing, probably enchanted sword that hung on his hip, I would have thought he was a normal human. Come to think of it, he probably is a normal human—just one with training and a church backing him.

"My apologies, Templar Ignis," Alexa replied, turning slightly to offer him a half bow. She did not let go of my hand during this period though, her healing faith magic still stitching me together. Whether it was due to the lack of complete obeisance or the use of magic, I saw the Templar's eyes narrow.

"I am here to inform you about your trial regulations," Ignis said.

"That was fast," Alexa said, eyes wide.

"Is this how you speak to a Templar, Initiate? You have not been away from the camp that long, have you?" Again, the Templar's voice came with a snap.

"My apologies, Templar Ignis," Alexa replied, bowing again. Her fingers around my hand clenched slightly as she did so, the flow of magic stuttering for a second.

"Better. Due to the circumstances of your *situation*, it has been decided your trial should be modified as you were informed. You and your sorcerer will both participate in the trial. To make it fairer, you will have a broader list of requirements to fulfill." Ignis reached a hand into his jacket, and he pulled an envelope out, then tossed it toward Alexa. It landed on the ground gently, part of it staining with blood immediately.

I found myself flashing Ignis a toothy grin, as his provocation did not result in Alexa letting go of my hand.

"You have two weeks."

"Thank you, Templar," Alexa said and bowed once more.

"Hey!" I called out. When Ignis turned toward me, I continued. "What makes you think I'm going along with this?"

"You will not aid your friend?"

"You mean the person you sent to guard me without my say-so? The one who has orders to take my head if I look like I might end up going over to the dark side, ring be damned?" I asked. I stared straight at Ignis when I said the second part, but I watched Alexa from the corner of my eyes while doing so, seeing the slight flinch and feeling a sudden increase in pressure on my hand. So. I was right.

"What do you want, sorcerer?"

"Mage. And I get paid for completing quests," I said, pointing to the birds around us. "Two weeks at my usual rate sounds just about right."

Ignis stared at me, his lip curling upward in a sneer. After a moment, he jerkily nodded and turned away. I couldn't help but flash a smile. When Ignis had walked away far enough, I hissed at Alexa. "You can stop squeezing so hard."

"Oh!" Alexa blushed slightly in embarrassment, releasing her death grip on my arm.

I growled as the magic slowly tapered off. I pulled my hand back, flexing it slightly, and marveled at the crusty wound. It looked like it had undergone weeks of healing in minutes, hints of new flesh showing under the scabbed-over wound.

"Don't do that!" Alexa said, smacking my picking fingers and making me wince. Unlike my own general healing spell, hers was more directed, which meant the major damage I had taken was healed over, but the rest of my body still ached from the myriad of cuts. With a grimace, I walked to my bag and returned with the first-aid kit to start working on our minor wounds. Iodine, antibiotic cream, and gauze... lots of gauze.

"So, he was nice," I said softly once we had the majority of our wounds taken care of and wrapped. Both of us had some form of additional healing speed—mine from Lily, and Alexa's… well, Alexa's from her faith in God, I guess, but it would do us no good to bleed out beforehand. Or, you know, get pulled over by the police for bleeding everywhere.

"Templar Ignis is extremely strict," Alexa said neutrally.

"Still watching us, eh?" I shook my head. Still, there were some advantages to them watching. Among other things, the wards helped ensure that our fight in a semi-popular park in the early hours of the morning had not drawn attention.

"Most likely," Alexa said. "Come, we should rest."

"And then we'll talk about how I've been shanghaied into this?" I asked as we limped back toward her car. Our bags dangled from our hands, the letter firmly stored in one of them.

"Well, you have been *paid* to do it," Alexa said snippily.

"Angry?" I asked. After a few paces of silence, I continued. "I'd have done it without the payment, but it is nice getting paid, no?"

"Would you? It's something you'd do for a friend," Alexa said, turning to look at me, her blue eyes troubled. "I'm just your *guard*, aren't I?"

"Guard and friend," I said, shrugging blithely. "You can be both."

"Can I?" Alexa breathed her words out, her voice troubled. But this time, I did not answer her.

After all, I'd said what I said. The rest, she would have to decide.

After a time, I raised my voice and said, "It's a murder. A murder of crows."

Chapter 4

"I'm not sure I should be letting Alexa choose your quests any longer," Lily said after I'd caught a quick shower and nap. Thankfully, the painkillers and nap had taken the edge off my headache. Now it just felt like a day-old caffeine headache. The three of us were now back in our sparsely furnished living room, clean and looking better off. Still, healing required food, and thus we were holding this meeting over the remnants of three large pizzas. Hawaiian for me, a meat lover's for Alexa, and a custom seafood, vegetable, and salami mix for Lily.

I laughed softly and shifted gingerly in my chair, my injured arm gently cradled in the other. "We are still getting the experience rewards, right?"

"And the money," Alexa confirmed while Lily sighed and waved her hand.

Quest complete! You successfully murdered the murder of Mystic Crows.

+187 XP

PS: Not all subjugation quests have to be finished with violence.

I laughed at Lily's note but had to admit the jinn had a point. Then again, Alexa had not been particularly interested in talking. Still, while being a murderhobo was all well and good in roleplaying games, running around killing everything you saw and stealing from every unlocked door was a good way to end up in jail in the real world.

"Well, the next few we don't have much choice on," I said, glancing at the blood-stained envelope and the pieces of paper that it once held. Lily sniffed at my words, glaring at the paper. After a moment, new notifications flashed in front of me.

New Quest Accepted – Help Alexa Complete Her Squire Trials (Chained Quest)

This is a chained quest. You must complete the sub-quests to complete the major quest.

Sub-quests:

- *Investigate and deal with the sudden influx of Leprechaun's Foot*
- *Collect fifty specimens of Spotted Wynn Mushrooms*
- *Deal with the issues plaguing the Brixton Orphanage*

"Is this normal?" I asked quietly, staring at the three tasks. Considering what she had said, I expected something a little bloodier. And rote. Other than the Wynn Mushrooms, most of these looked rather specific to our city.

"No," Alexa said simply. "Normally it's more to deal with a haunting or killing a few undead. Maybe travel to Africa and kill a few shifters."

"Wait, you kill shifters?" I asked, disapproval in my voice. "I thought—"

"They were civilized? Most are, but there are roaming mercenary groups of shifters in Africa who offer their services to various warlords. And who don't bother asking the populace their thoughts when they recruit new members." Alexa's face darkened. "You'd be surprised how many charitable Christian missions include a class of initiates on their class test."

"I… see." I prodded at my own feelings, trying to decide how I felt about sending a bunch of teenagers out on a kill mission, and I found I truly had very little objections. It didn't seem that different from the government doing the same. At least in this case, they were going after known assholes. Or so I hoped.

"Guess we're special," I said, rubbing my chin. "Which one do you think we should tackle first?"

"Why don't we split it?" Alexa said, tapping the air in front of her before realizing I could not see what she saw. Being part of my party, Lily had shared a stripped-down version of my notification screen with Alexa. The party screen and Alexa's health gauge were two of the things that the wish benefitted the initiate directly on. "I'll visit the orphanage, and you talk to El about where you can find Wynn Mushrooms."

"El probably would know if anyone does," I said, agreeing with Alexa. El was my pixie friend, a used clothing shopkeeper I had known before the change. The pixie's other, less public job was buying and selling alchemical and enchantment ingredients for the supernatural population. "But it won't take me very long to finish with El. So why don't I meet you at the orphanage? That way you can meet with them first anyway."

Alexa's lips pursed and for a moment. I wondered if she didn't want me to visit the orphanage. After all, I was an evil sorcerer, at least to some strict interpretations. It'd bitten us in the ass a few times before.

"Okay," Alexa said after a moment, seeming to have come to a decision. We continued to chat for a bit, Lily providing a little more background on the mushrooms, which—I was unhappy to learn—were not known to grow in clumps. In fact, the magical mushrooms grew and thrived in areas of intense emotion. As for Leprechaun's Foot, either the jinn really knew nothing or felt it was better for us to learn about it ourselves. Myself, I was pretty sure it was the second option.

***

As usual, the window display at Nora's, El's shop, had changed again, filled with a tasteful and colorful ensemble of clothing on mannequins. The display mostly focused on women's clothing, though I did see a particular hipster ensemble with a hat, skinny pants, and a fringed jean shirt that made my lips quirk. Then again, I was wearing a shirt that had Han Solo saying: "Make it so." Perhaps critiquing other people's fashion choices might not be my best move.

Inside Nora's was the usual cluster of used clothing racks, carefully laid out to allow shoppers to browse in peace while allowing El to watch everyone. It even had a few safety mirrors set up, though only after my transformation did I notice they had been enchanted to strip away enchantments from the reflections. At least, for those who had the eyes to see.

El herself was busy at one corner of the counter, working through a pile of clothing brought in by one of her irregular "suppliers." Like myself, before my wish, they had deposited an eclectic mix of clothing purchased at garage sales, other used stores, eBay, and storage auctions. Rather than bother El, I browsed the store myself until she was free.

"Henry," El called. Out of the corner of my eyes, I saw her nod at me, and for a second, I had a sense of vertigo. At first, she looked like the matronly older woman I had known for years, a hefty brunette who always had a kind smile and an ability to pay more than other stores. Then, the flame-haired, slim beauty appeared as I stared at the pixie head-on, her glamour falling away under my Mage Sight.

"Hey, El," I greeted her, walking toward the counter.

"Here to buy or sell?" El asked.

"I could be asking for work," I replied with a smile. In my earlier days, El had kindly provided me a series of jobs collecting various enchanted material from around the city. It was low-paying work, but it was work I could manage at my lower level. Since I'd gained Alexa's help and leveled up, I'd been here much less often.

"I wish," El said with a smile. "You were one of my best suppliers, but sending a mage to collect Grimmark Gum might be overkill."

"Probably," I said, repressing my curiosity about what Grimmark Gum was. Getting into a discussion about it would eat up most of the afternoon. It was no surprise that with El's extensive knowledge of materials she had done as well as she had in the mystical ingredient business. The sale of her used clothing basically acted as her cover and allowed her to launder her earnings.

"Actually, I need some advice. I've got to collect some spotted Wynn mushrooms," I said, rubbing my nose. "Lily filled us in a bit on them, but I figured you might know…"

"Where to find it in the city?" El finished my sentence before she nodded slowly. "I know a few places, but the spotted Wynn are rare. How many do you need?"

"Fifty."

"Fifty?" El squeaked slightly, shaking her head rapidly. "What are you trying to do? Lay the entire New York undead population to rest?"

"Pardon?" I asked. "Isn't the mushroom for Mana recovery?"

"Wynn mushrooms are enhancers. Spotted Wynn are ten times more effective. Your Templar friends use it quite often in their censers when they do battle with the undead," El said. "They use it to disrupt their attachment to this world, and against weaker undead, it can even send them directly back."

"Oh." I frowned. Huh. "How much do they use?"

"I'm not sure, but generally about half a mushroom is enough for a single censer. You'd be collecting enough for a hundred censers, and those burn for a good hour or so," El replied.

"So, locations?" I asked after a moment. After all, it didn't matter what I wanted. What I needed was fifty specimens.

"I'm not sure," El said. "I can point you to a few locations, but Jordie's my mushroom man. He'd know better."

"Think you could put me in touch with him?" I asked after consideration. I understood El not knowing exact locations. In fact… "Do you have any in stock?"

"I could, but Jordie's not exactly the most talkative. But I've got two in stock right now," El said, eyeing me. "Link?"

"Yeah, Link spell. If Jordie doesn't work…" I shrugged. El knew enough of my abilities to know what I was going to do.

"Fine. But only once, you hear me? No collecting otherwise. And I'm going to charge you a premium," El said threateningly.

"Done." I sighed. I understood her point. Having a mage like me going around sweeping up all the alchemical ingredients was rather unfair—on her business and her collectors' livelihoods. It was one thing for me to be working as a collector for her, another to be hogging all the ingredients. The only reason mages didn't do it more often was that there was no point. Generally, most mages had better things to do with their time.

Then again, most mages weren't penniless cheats like me.

"Oh, before I forget. Leprechaun's Foot. Ever heard of it?" I asked El, recalling the other quest. We hadn't even made plans to deal with it, not knowing what exactly it was.

"Why do you want to know?" El said, her tone suddenly serious.

"Quest," I said.

El eyed me, her green-and-blue eyes hard and serious as they fixed on my face, searching for a lie that did not exist. After a moment, she relaxed and nodded. "Stay away from using it. It's bad news of the worse kind."

"But what is it?"

"Leprechaun's Foot is a luck drug. It alters your luck for the better," El said, her lips tight. "It's an old formula, renamed a few times. Karma's

Whore, the Devil's Gift, Norn's Blessing. It's had a lot of names but the same formula."

"I take it there's something wrong with the way it's made?"

"Luck. Fate. Karma. However you call it, we all have some aspect of fortune provided to us, gifted if you will, from our past lives. The Foot, it requires taking from one to another, but there's no way to take, to remove such a thing without harming the original host. And the price paid by those taking it in the future is even greater," El said.

"Rule of three?" I asked curiously. It was something the Mage Council scoffed at officially but that individuals from the older traditions believed in, in one form or another. The rule of three itself was from Wicca, the belief that any magic used returned threefold. Good or bad. Which of course encouraged Wiccans to use it for good. For many supernaturals, whether it was karma or fate, the belief in old traditions certainly held true and guided their actions to some extent.

"Yes."

I paused then, somewhat awkwardly. My next question was self-evident, but it could so easily be misconstrued.

"You want to know how it's made." El read me like a book.

"Yeah," I replied softly. "Can't track it without, well…"

"No," El replied flatly. "I won't help you on that."

"Figured," I said with a sigh. Damn it. Still, if it was a drug, I knew a few people. Which amused me in a way. I knew how to get an illegal supernatural drug but had not a clue where I would purchase a bag of marijuana. Tells you the kind of life I led these days.

"Henry, be careful," El said sternly. "The type of people who make these kinds of drugs, they're not the kind you cross."

I nodded, stories of Mexican drug cartels flashing through my mind. I really didn't want my house burned down, my hands chopped off, and my balls stuffed into my mouth. Not in that order necessarily. "I'll be careful."

El sighed at my words, and I bid her goodbye. At least, to some extent, Alexa and I were protected by my wish, but there were so many loopholes in the wish that it was scant protection if someone really desired our deaths. Still, it wasn't as if we could say no. With troubled thoughts about my future and the potential for mayhem in my life, I flagged down a taxi to bring me to the orphanage.

***

The orphanage itself was a squat grey building, probably built in the sixties when the greatest architectural dream of the masses was cheap, grey, and functional. Frankly, it was depressing even looking at it, but it was functional. The murals the young children had painted on the side of the building and the well-tended flower boxes added a touch of life and color to it, that and the large—for an inner-city building—green grounds surrounding its fenced exterior. Only a small sign over the door, right below the address marker, spoke of the Brixton Orphanage's purpose.

Still, located as it was on the outskirts of downtown, flanked by tall glass buildings filled with yuppies, club kids, and the nouveau rich, I could start making assumptions about some of Brixton's troubles. The nun who let me in and had me wait in the foyer for Alexa was charming and kind but firm in keeping me from heading deeper into the building itself. Which was fine by me as it left me time to speculate if this orphanage was another feeder location for initiates. Who was I kidding? They all probably were.

I turned my thoughts over in my mind for a bit, considering how I felt about an organization that went about recruiting children to become trained killers. Generally, this was something heavily frowned upon, an act that was derided the world over for removing the "innocence" of a child. Then again, from the little I'd been told by Alexa, it wasn't as if they were making the children kill immediately. That was generally left until they were in their teens, about the same age as we'd let others go to war. It was just that the initiates had a much longer training time, and it wasn't as if they couldn't back out if they wanted to.

Then again, if all you knew was a certain lifestyle, how easy was it to leave? Cults the world over used the exclusion of the outside world to brainwash and restrict their people, ensuring loyalty. Was what the Templars doing that different? Does intent and good intentions matter when the actions themselves aren't necessarily good?

"Henry?" Alexa called to me. She walked out of the office and caught me seated on a wooden bench, thinking uncharitable thoughts of her people.

I stood as I greeted her. "Alexa. How are you doing?"

"Good. I've cleared it with the abbess for you to come in farther," Alexa said.

"So what's the problem here?"

"Two things. Firstly, they have a problem with a local developer. He keeps trying to pressure the orphanage to sell. The orphanage has barely been keeping afloat with the rising property taxes in the last few years, but the government inspectors have been coming by more regularly, fining them for the smallest infractions. Last week, the building inspectors came by for a "routine" inspection and cited a number of code requirements they had to meet—requirements they had been allowed to bypass as they were grandfathered in."

I frowned, cocking my head to the side.

"Yes, it's not normal. They're pretty sure the building inspectors and others have been paid off."

"Who?" I asked, curiously.

"The developer is named Connor Weeks," Alexa said as she led me down the quiet hallways. I was surprised that for such a large building supposedly filled with kids, it was so silent. Then again, I guessed it was class time or something. Soon enough, we arrived at a staircase which Alexa took downward, leading me toward the basement. "In either case, the orphanage began the process of having contractors come in to get back up to code and—"

"And ran into something weird," I said, finishing for her. When we exited the stairway, we entered a simple stone corridor. Immediately, I could feel the slight vibrations in mana that ran through the orphanage grow even more powerful while the small and discreet runic carvings hidden among the stonework seemed even more populous here. I grimaced, reaching out to touch one of the runes. Alexa said nothing, waiting as I let my eyes defocus slightly and traced the flow of mana through the orphanage. It took minutes before I was certain, but when I was done, I knew for sure.

"The contractors broke the runes."

"They did," Alexa said and pointed down one of the corridors. I followed the lady with the directions silently, continuing to sense the mana flow, which seemed disturbed by light touches of something darker, more bestial in it. Not human for sure. But at least it wasn't demonic.

"Do you have a feeling like they want you to fail?" I asked absently.

"Why would you say that?" Alexa said as we started spotting more and more signs of work half started and abandoned. The various construction workhorses, plywood, and tools left abandoned.

"Really? There's no way you'd be able to complete the second quest without me in two weeks, not with everything else. And as for this one…" I sighed. "It doesn't seem like something a typical squire would be expected to do."

"It isn't," Alexa said. "But then, I'm not your typical initiate, am I?"

"No, I guess not."

We finally made it to the end of the corridor, coming to what looked like a simple storage room to the untrained eye, but I noticed the numerous runic carvings over the door and along the hallway arches, some of them now marred and broken. I had to frown as some runes, even untouched, had lost their glow, seeming to have faded in their usability. "What's in there?"

"Storeroom," Alexa said and opened the door. The blonde began to step in and then visibly hesitated, her brows creasing together. "What?"

"You feel it too," I stated and pushed past her to step within. I ignored the way the hair on the back of my neck stood up, the way my stomach roiled when I walked in. I felt my muscles tensing, my shoulders tightening, and my breath shortening as an existential dread filled me. The room itself was an empty storage room, nothing to mark it from any other room except for the small runic carvings lining the ceiling and floor. Except, a number of these carvings were chipped. I stood within the room in silence, tracing the flow of mana within.

"What do you see?"

"Unlike outside, where the runes, the ritual are all passive and part of one massive spell, there are actually multiple spells here. There's a glamour hiding the majority of these runes from sight, but it has been damaged," I said, pointing to runes as I spoke. "And there's another runic set taking the ambient mana in to power these runes along with the mana that the external runes feed it. But on top of that, there's a containment rune too. These rituals…"

"Yes?" Alexa prompted me.

"They're out of my ballpark. They're significantly more complex than anything I know," I admitted. "I'd need to do some studying before I could even hope to fix this."

Alexa grimaced, but, seeing I was done with the room, happily stepped out. The moment we left, she began to relax slightly like I did. Even then, I sensed that the leakage of mana and, for want of a better word, intent from the failed containment runes were beginning to permeate the air.

"Is it dangerous?"

"Not in the short term," I said, tapping my lips. "I wouldn't necessarily want to be here in a few months, but the containment spell is chipped, not broken."

"Good," Alexa said.

"So how do we want to do this?" I asked, gesturing within. "That's a big job, but we've got two other quests to handle too."

"Let's start on the mushrooms first," Alexa finally said after some consideration. "We can work on it immediately while we brainstorm about the dual problem. I'll ask the abbess to have the contractors work on other areas for now, and we'll try to figure out what to do about Weeks. As for the drug, we'll need a sample of the Foot if what you told me is true."

"There might be someone I know," I said slowly, thinking of Andy. The orc lived in the right neighborhood, and I'd run into him a few times while doing deliveries for El. While he preferred to keep things "clean" with protection rackets, gambling, and gun running, he was in the "life" as it were. Of course, Alexa looked at me strangely, but for once, I decided not to answer her. Sometimes, it was good to be mysterious.

Chapter 5

Hunting down magic mushrooms was, frankly, a rather boring task. The challenge in acquiring the mushrooms was in the quantity required. Each location we hit only had one such stalk, which was often surrounded by other, non-spotted varieties. Of course, since we were penniless drones, we scooped up the non-spotted varieties as well while we were at it, but at the end of the day, we'd only managed to get half a dozen stalks. Most of the day itself was spent in transit as my magic led us from spot to spot. Picking the mushrooms themselves was relatively simple as their defense mechanism was passive, forcing most supernaturals to ignore them.

At this rate, collecting the mushrooms seemed to be an easily doable quest requiring only a few days. Except this was the start. Each mushroom spot was quite close together, easy to reach, but as we harvested more and more, we'd be forced to travel farther and farther, adding to the time taken. And of course, we had another pair of quests to deal with. Still, of the three quests, this seemed to be the easiest, even if it was somewhat draining for me to constantly keep Link active.

The next morning, I brought Alexa with me when I visited Andy. This time we were headed to the southwestern part of the city, where the old docks lay rotting. Without the constant flow of business, the neighborhood was a mixture of rundown warehouses, squat concrete buildings, and crumbling docks along with a few over-burdened homeless shelters. Dotted throughout the neighborhood were failed attempts at revitalization, the scenic concrete-and-grass walkways along the river unkept and littered with debris, a pair of soaring condos looming over their older cousins. It was, frankly, where I'd expect the sale of Leprechaun's Foot to do the best.

When we pulled into the neighborhood in Alexa's tiny hatchback, we received more than one interested look from the neighborhood's denizens. Hunched over, hooded figures slunk from corner to corner, hands in baggy clothing, maybe one in eight of them sporting inhuman features—snouts, whiskers, fur, and more. The others, the human denizens, were your mixture of the homeless, the working poor, the downtrodden, and the Samaritans who worked these streets. No big surprise that the pair of us—Alexa in particular with her good looks and muscular body—drew so much attention.

"You sure my car is going to be okay here?" Alexa asked softly, eyeing the individuals around us a bit worriedly. While the car itself had been mildly reinforced with a few enchantments, it was only mildly. After all, the kinds of questions you'd get for driving around with the enchanted equivalent of a tank was not worth the marginal increase in protection most of the time. It wasn't as if our lives involved car-chase scenes with machine guns spraying bullets everywhere.

"It will be," I said, looking around until I spotted a familiar face. I waved the slouching orc over, him glaring at me with the solemn defiance of a teenager. "Want to earn fifty bucks?"

"You want me to watch the *chica*'s wheels?" The teenage orc slurred, giving Alexa an obvious once-over. I watched Alexa straighten slightly, anger flickering in her eyes.

"Do that again, and it's forty." I pulled out a twenty and waved it in front of the kid. "Twenty now, the rest once we get back and the car's in one piece."

"You going to see Andy?" the kid asked, eyeing the money with interest.

"Yup."

"Okay." The kid nodded and snatched the twenty from me. Afterward, he moved over to slouch on the car itself, glowering at everyone who looked at it. As Alexa eyed me dubiously, I grabbed her arm and dragged her along.

"You sure—"

"He's just a visible marker. Now that people know we're visiting Andy, they won't touch your car," I explained softly as we walked down the street to where the orc ganger normally hung out. His stoop with his buddies, if you will.

"Are you going to tell me who we're meeting?" Alexa asked after a while.

"Patience, padawan," I said with a chuckle. When we turned the corner, I spotted a group of orcs hanging out beneath the rectangular apartment building, chatting and drinking. Out of curiosity, I eyed the street, grateful to not see any police presence here. Of course, with the way the police patrolled the streets, you never knew when things might change. As we neared the group, an orc ran in our direction but came to a stop when he noticed the pair of us.

"Henry." Andy greeted me with a toothy, tusky smile. Amusingly enough, orcs in this world came in a variety of forms. Green and grey skin, big and small tusks, with overhung foreheads and more "human" miens, there seemed to be a variety of them. Truth be told, they had distinctive species traits, but because we could, humanity had lumped them all together as orcs and called it a day. And because they were lumped together, they had decided to group together themselves. And so, the group before me was a wide variety of orcs, arising from different locations of the world. Really, only a nerd like me would recall their species' traits. After all, for someone like the Templars, all they needed to know was that the orcs bled like humans.

"Andy," I replied, gesturing back toward Alexa. "This is Alexa. She's a friend of mine."

Andy nodded slowly, eyeing the muscular blonde. His friends had parted when we arrived, the group letting us in and surrounding us in a loose semicircle now. This made Alexa tense slightly, a hand resting on her pocket where I knew she carried her extendable baton. Still, no one was drawing which was a win, at least for me so far.

"Well, if you're vouching for her…"

"I am. We aren't here for long. I just need some minor help," I said and smiled slightly at the orc.

"Har. The mage needs our help. Need someone beaten down? An office ransacked?" Andy leered at me, and for a moment, I could not tell if he was pulling my leg or actually offering— which, come to think of it, might've been the point.

"Nothing of the sort. Well, maybe a little," I said, considering what I wanted. "I'm looking for a sample of Leprechaun's Foot. Actually, possibly more than one."

The moment the drug's name hit the air, the atmosphere changed. The casual friendliness and ribbing disappeared, the group tensing around us while Andy's eyes narrowed.

"Why are you looking for that, Henry?" Andy asked, his voice a low growl. "You ain't going to use it, are you?"

"Not ingesting it," I said, raising my hands quickly as if to ward off his words. "I've got a quest, to look into the sudden increase of it on the streets. I can Link the samples, maybe get some research done then."

"So your first instinct is to buy some illegal drugs."

"Uhhh—"

"Rather than say, talk to us?" Andy asked angrily.

"Oh. Ummm—"

"Mages!" Andy harrumphed angrily and then shook his head. "The Foot's coming down from the Skulls. Green Skulls."

"Green Skulls?" I frowned.

There was a loud sigh from one of Andy's friends, who got shut down by a look from Andy, but even the orc leader seemed slightly exasperated with me. "They're another supernatural gang, werejackal based. They've been peddling that garbage for the last few weeks and expanding their base of operations aggressively. We've had a few clashes in the last few days."

"Huh," I said slowly, then glanced at Alexa for a moment. She shrugged her shoulders, a gesture I couldn't actually read. Still, I saw no reason for Andy to lie to us, so I probed for a little more, getting what information we could before we were quietly "escorted" back to our car. It was only when we were in the car itself when Alexa spoke again.

"That was… different," the initiate said.

"Oh?"

"They were a lot politer than I expected. And helpful."

"If the Green Skulls are after their streets, I'm not surprised," I said softly, rubbing my chin. "Andy's not a huge fan of people moving in on them."

"Perhaps," Alexa said doubtfully. "But are you sure they aren't lying to you?"

"For what?"

"To point you at an enemy? An enraged mage can do a lot of damage."

"Andy wouldn't—" I paused, then sighed. "Fine. He might. But I wasn't planning on going in guns blazing."

"How were you planning this?"

I paused, considering. "Maybe we should grab a cup of coffee and talk about this."

"You think?" Alexa asked with a snort.

She guided the car toward the curb when we found a coffee shop. Yeah, perhaps some planning made sense.

***

Once we had the basics of a plan down, we put it into action. We faced a few problems. Firstly, while I didn't have an outsized reputation, I had gained some notoriety in town. There just weren't that many competent mages, and even fewer willing to do work for those not swimming in cash. It meant I couldn't exactly saunter into the middle of Green Skulls territory without potentially being spotted. Alexa herself was not much better—even if no one realized she was an initiate, she was, for all intents and purposes, a mundane.

The first step then was a glamour. Unlike illusions that were static projections which altered how they looked in reality—like holographic projections—glamours worked on an individual's mind. Because illusions worked on reality, they were harder to control and thus mostly utilized on static objects, while glamours were much simpler. Unfortunately, because they affected an individual's mind, it was also easier to beat in some ways. Someone particularly perceptive, awakened, or mindful of their thoughts could beat a glamour. It was the reason why, even without trying, my mage sight cut through most glamours and showed me the true face of individuals around us.

To cast a glamour that "beat" whatever was out there, I needed to take more care and put more *oomph* than the stock enchantments peddled by apprentice mages and sorcerers on street corners. Thankfully, my glamour spell was significantly better than what most enchantments were made from, Lily having scoffed at the current state of the industry. Then again, most glamour spells were meant to deceive mundanes.

"You sure this will work?" Alexa muttered as we walked through the rundown neighborhood later that day.

Unlike the docks, the Green Skulls had a more prosperous neighborhood under their thumb, even if prosperous was a matter of degrees. Buildings here mostly had their windows in one piece, even if graffiti was everywhere and trash accumulated around us. Unlike the docks, the homeless were fewer here, their presence less desirable. On most street corners, we noted young men standing around taking cash, while children ran the goods to customers, and prostitutes smiled and strutted their stuff along the streets.

"The glamours will hold," I muttered through the corner of my mouth softly. We both had changed our clothing to something a little more worn—and less geeky in my case—courtesy of a thrift store. Both of us wore baggy hoodies, Alexa to hide her fit figure and mine to hide my skinny one. "We're just looking for now. Maybe grab a cup of coffee…" I said softly, jerking my head to the lone diner that sat on the corner.

Alexa made a face at my suggestion but shifted her trajectory slightly as we headed toward the diner. Unlike most other corners, this one was empty, bereft of drug dealers, though we passed by enough on our walk and heard their "recommendations." Sadly, we heard nothing similar to what we wanted, declining offers for marijuana, crack, and other "mundane" drugs. But at least I now had an idea of where to pick those up.

Once inside the diner, we found ourselves a seat in one of the duct-taped polystyrene booths and waited to be served. And waited. And waited. Thankfully, we weren't particularly concerned with the lack of service while we took note of the rest of the diners.

An old man sat at the bar with a plate of pie and a newspaper before him. A trio of hookers chatted quietly among themselves as they took a few minutes to relax and massage tired feet. A tired, overweight waitress in her worn uniform of pale blue and white smoked a cigarette right under the No Smoking sign. And of course, a large grouping of werejackals sat at the opposite end of the diner, their bodies in human form but shimmering with the slight hazy outline of their hybrid form behind them—at least to my eyes.

Alexa noted my gaze but didn't turn around, instead pulling the steel napkin dispenser to play around with—and, of course, adjusting it enough to glance behind her. After a few minutes, she twisted around and spotted the waitress to meet her eyes directly. With a huff, the waitress walked to our table and slapped down a pair of menus before sauntering away.

"Well, she's not getting a tip," I said with a sigh before perusing the menu. I frowned, suddenly stumped, when I realized I had no way to listen to the group speak. And speaking they were certainly doing.

"The menu's not that bad," Alexa said, mistaking my frown.

"No… just…" I sighed, then shook my head. Right. The movies always made this entire "gather intel" thing so much easier than it was. They always had the right tool for the situation, the luck to meet the right person, the skills to do it right. But here I was, sitting in a diner under a glamour that made me look like just another human, and I had no idea what to do next. I couldn't hear them speak, and I couldn't cast Link without risking them sensing my use of active magic. We could, at best, see them make a deal or two, and what would that tell us? Nothing more than what Andy already had.

"Just relax," Alexa said softly, flashing me a slight smile.

"Okay…" I sighed and closed my mouth. She was right. We had talked about this. We were only here to watch. Everything else—anything else— we learned was a bonus.

***

An hour later, after a rather unsatisfactory, sloppy burger and over-cooked fries, the pair of us finally left the diner. We'd dragged out the meal as long as we could—inadvertently helped by the lousy service—but now, we needed to leave. Either that or attract more attention to us than we wanted.

In that time, we'd learned all of nothing. That wasn't exactly true of course. We had spotted a few members of the Green Skulls. We knew what they liked to eat and that they enjoyed hanging out at the diner. In fact, it was interesting to note that the vast majority of the gang must have been men; no women had been present at the diner. Of course, there were other reasons for that. The way they'd interacted with the ladies of the night was a pretty good reason why no sensible woman would want to be around them. But in the end, it was still not particularly useful information.

When we'd left, it was alone. I clocked the pair of werejackals who came out a short couple of seconds after us but thought nothing of it. Not until I noticed they took the same corner as we did, their pace slowly increasing.

"Trouble," I said softly to Alexa.

"I noticed. Confront or run?" Alexa said.

"That…" I frowned, considering the matter. I shot her a look back in question, dithering.

"Too late." Alexa pointed subtly ahead.

I looked up and noticed another pair of werejackals, these two not even bothering to hide the fact they were coming for us. "This way."

Alexa grabbed my arm and tugged me sideways, pulling me down an alleyway. A quick look around showed us it was filled with a pair of foul-smelling garbage dumpsters, soiled clothing, and other unmentionable wastes. A single, huddled body in the corner indicated the alleyway wasn't as empty as we wished, but at least it was out of sight.

"Watch our back," Alexa said as she reached behind her and pulled her baton out. She kept it in her hand, unextended for now as she waited. It wasn't a long wait before the quartet of werejackals made their appearance with wide, almost lolling grins on their faces.

"Hello there, girlie. So nice of you to stop." One of the werejackals walked forward, a loose, cloth jacket in red and white hanging over tattered blue jeans. Obviously, he was the leader – of this group at the least if not the whole group.

"What do you want?" Alexa asked.

"Just a word," the werejackal said. "You and your boy were real curious about us. We're not real friendly with new strangers…"

"Don't know what you're talking about," Alexa said softly.

"Really. Then why'd you run?"

"Two big men chasing us down? Seemed like a good idea."

"Really? That what you think too, boy? You going to let the girlie talk for you?" the werejackal asked, taunting me.

"Yes," I said simply. With my body bladed toward the group, I could watch both sides of the alleyway, with most of my attention facing behind us. It meant I saw the van pull up at the end of the alleyway first.

"More company," I whispered softly to Alexa.

"Damn." Alexa set her feet apart and reached with her other hand into her jacket pocket. She froze when the lead jackal pulled out a gun and aimed it at her. Within seconds, the other werejackals had pulled out various weapons.

"Easy there, girlie. We don't want any mistakes," the werejackal said.

Alexa pressed her lips together but slowly eased her hand away from her hoodie. I grimaced, mentally running our options through my mind. I could throw up a Mana Shield, and it could deflect some bullets, but the sheer number and the fact that they had us flanked made it a bad option. Fighting them, well, that probably would just result in our deaths. Or severe injury at the least.

"That's better. Now, why don't you tell us the real reason you're here."

I frowned, my mind racing as I looked for a way out. Damn it, this damn quest, this confrontation was unwinnable. No competent game master would ever let you run into a situation like this. There's no way to fight…

"I told you—" Alexa paused when I laid my hand on her arm. She shot me a quizzical look that held traces of "what the hell are you doing" in it.

"Fine. I'll tell you the truth," I said, stepping forward slightly and past Alexa. When the werejackal focused on me, I continued and desperately hoped I was right. "My name is Henry Tsien. I'm the new mage."

Hisses and growls erupted from the werejackals as even more weapons pointed toward me.

I ignored them, even as I felt my back grow cold and clammy from sweat. "I have a quest."

"Better." The werejackal grinned, staring at me. "So, you meaning to mess with the Skulls? If you do, you'd be dull." Laughter erupted at that, the sing-song manner the werejackal said the last line an indicator he had probably said this a million times before.

"No. I'm here to collect mushrooms," I said. When the laughter finally died down, I gestured to my backpack. "If you'll let me, I'll show you."

"Slowly."

"Of course," I said. It did not take me long to take out my sample and show them the spotted Wynn I had collected. "These are spotted Wynn. They're good money if you can collect them, but they're rare." I noticed one of the werejackals leaning in and whispering to the lead one, but I ignored it, continuing my story. "We came here to check out this area because we heard you ran this neighborhood. Since poaching is bad…" I trailed off, shrugging my shoulders.

"You wanted to see if you could get away with it." The werejackal snarled at me.

"No. I wanted to assess your gang, see if the rumors about your drug dealing were true. If you did deal drugs, you wouldn't want to deal with a mage over a couple of mushrooms," I said simply. "I doubt the number we could scavenge here would be worth even a quarter of your night's revenue."

"Damn right," one of the other werejackals boasted before he got smacked over the back of his head by another.

"And that's the truth, is it, mage?" the leader asked, walking forward. I sensed Alexa tensing behind me, but I held my hand out backward, hoping she got the meaning. *Stand down*. We couldn't win a fight here.

"Yes," I said simply.

"See… There's only one problem with that." I found myself tensing when the werejackal neared, his face scrunching up while his gun continued to point at the middle of my chest.

"Oh?" I focused, building a Force Shield spell in my mind, holding it in abeyance for the moment.

"Yes. You smell crafty," the werejackal said, his eyes glinting as he stopped a few short feet from me.

"Well, I am a mage," I said, cursing inside. Of course. He was a shifter. Expanded senses were one of the major things they all had. Still, I had chosen my words carefully to tell the truth. Just not all of it. I just hoped it had been sufficient.

The werejackal paused for a second at my answer, then burst out laughing. It wasn't a normal laugh, more like a braying, yowling noise. A few seconds later, all his friends joined in, making the hair at the back of my neck stand even straighter. If it wasn't for the fact they'd lowered their guns when they laughed, I'd be even more worried. But still, guns were still in their hands, so I kept a close eye on them. When the laughter finally subsided, the leader stared at me again, pointing his gun back at my chest.

"Funny. Funny mage. Okay. You smell somewhat truthful. And they say don't mess with mages, so we won't. But I don't want to see your faces here again either," the werejackal said, gesturing with his gun to the side in an obvious invitation for us to leave.

I nodded and waved Alexa ahead of me. We skirted to the side of the alleyway, and the pair of us slowly shuffled past the werejackals who barely moved far enough aside to let us through. I kept myself in front of Alexa, my ability to put the primed and ready Force Shield in front of us at a moment's notice a better option than anything she could do. It seemed she agreed since I didn't get a complaint. Still, other than a sudden lunging motion by one werejackal—which managed to elicit a slight jerk from me—and a series of cackling laughter by the werejackals, they let us leave.

It was only when we finally got back to Alexa's car and were blocks away that we began to relax. I shuddered then, the adrenaline slowly leaving my body as my hands shook and too-tense muscles around my neck unclenched. I groaned softly, waiting for the after-battle effects to go away.

Damn it. That had been too damn close.

Chapter 6

We regrouped back at the duplex, safe behind magical wa—shit. I hadn't even managed to put those up. I buried my head in my hands again and forced myself to draw deep breaths. I felt my heart begin to jackhammer again. I'd risked my life before, nearly gotten killed, but somehow, staring down the end of a gunmetal barrel had driven home how little of a game this was, how pitiful my simple Force Shield was and how little it could do.

A low thump near my head had me raising it to stare at a slowly steaming cup of tea set on the coffee table, inviting me with its rich, creamy tones. I reached out, wincing slightly at the heat when I cupped the beverage in my hands and stared at Alexa, who sat across from me with her own cup.

"First. Tea? Don't you think I've been tortured enough? And secondly, how are you so calm?" I asked, at first trying for a joking tone before my voice rose at the end, escaping my control. I choked back my rising voice, drawing a deeper breath.

"Training," Alexa said simply, touching her cup to her lips before lowering it and staring at me. "Experience. Ritual. Mindfulness."

"Have I mentioned how messed up your childhood was?" I asked Alexa rhetorically. But thinking about her rather than my own reaction helped me push feelings of helplessness and rage away for a moment. I drew a breath, sitting up slightly more as I finally tasted my tea. "Ugh! What is this tea?"

"Peppermint. And you shouldn't be doing that," Alexa said.

"Doing what?" I stared at the abomination of liquid in my cup, debating why people would do this to themselves. What was wrong with simple black tea? Jasmine. Pu'er. Maybe a little dragon seed.

"Avoiding processing," Alexa said as she leaned forward, meeting my brown eyes with her blue ones. "If you have to, you have to, but we're safe. You should let yourself process your emotions. Otherwise, it'll affect your performance later."

"Performance…" I said softly, picking at her words. The initiate didn't flinch, just continued staring at me. I found myself looking away eventually, looking aside to stare at the jinn who was blatantly not listening in on us. "I just… I couldn't stop those bullets. Not even if I tried. A single Force Shield, at full strength, I could do if they were in front of us. Or behind. But if I had to split the spell, or dual cast… I don't think I could do it."

"It would have been difficult," Alexa replied.

"I felt like such a fraud. A mage. Who can't even throw lightning or fire properly. Who can't stop bullets. Who gets run off by a gang of thugs," I said softly, shaking my head. "And it was my idea to go in there, to look. Because I didn't know what else to do. I just feel so stupid."

"You're not stupid," Alexa said softly, reprimanding me. "You're just out of your depth. You're learning, but six months ago you had no idea of this world. For a civilian, you are doing amazingly well."

"Learning…" I sipped on my tea again and made a face, once again reminded about what I had in hand. "I keep doing this. Getting in over my head. Learning as I go along. Hoping I can cobble a solution together with whatever I have." I waved my hand at Lily before continuing. "We got away because I guessed it was a social confrontation, that if it wasn't, we'd have been warned. Or protected. But, maybe I—we… wouldn't.

"Because the wish I made had to be open, had to be vague, so Lily could fix things as they came up. But of course, she's limited too. I'm playing a game I can't read the rules of. There's no manual, and I was the guy who always RTFMed."

"RTFM?"

"Read the fucking manual," I replied. "But it's not a game because people die."

"No, it's not," Alexa said softly. "But it is your life."

I paused at her last words, drawing a deep shuddering breath. It was my life. And damn it, I had chosen it—chosen it and chosen that perhaps I would do something more than just live it for myself. So here I was, trying to help a friend, and not doing a good job at it. I shook my head, clutching my mug harder as my thoughts spiraled, as I searched for resolve and understanding within myself. Alexa stayed silent, sipping on her mug of tea while I worked through my emotions and the implications of her words.

"It is, isn't it?" I said softly. "Then perhaps I should stop playing…"

Alexa smiled softly, tilting her head to the side. I fell silent again, caught in my own thoughts. I was dimly aware Alexa stopped to whisper to Lily before she walked toward the stairs, pausing only long enough to place a hand on my shoulder as she left. When she did, I felt the warmth of her hand leave too, leaving me with my thoughts as the night deepened.

***

"Morning, Henry," Alexa said softly when she came downstairs the next day. I was seated on the couch, the discarded remnants of various sugary snacks scattered around me. I blinked, startling awake from the light doze I had fallen into and wincing when the stream of sunlight penetrated my eyes.

"Morning…" I grunted out, rubbing at my eyes.

"Did he not sleep?" Alexa asked.

"A bit, but he mostly sat there muttering to himself," Lily replied, looking up. I frowned, hating how she seemed to be still chipper and put together even after an all-night gaming session.

"Extra coffee then," Alexa said in reply, heading to the kitchen as she hid a light yawn behind her hand. "Should I call Caleb and let him know you'll be skipping his lesson?"

"No!" I shouted, jerking awake further. "No," I said again, more moderately. "I have questions and training I need to do."

"Oh?"

"I need to work on dual casting. Or a better shield. Or both." I spat out my reply quickly and then drew a deep breath before continuing. "Also, I think we're looking at these quests the wrong way. Or I am. I'm not playing the game right."

Alexa winced but did not stop her preparation of the coffee pot. The pot itself had been cleaned the day before, so it took her only a few seconds.

"Don't worry," I said. "I don't mean I'm thinking it's a game but that the way I've been approaching this has been wrong. I've been so caught up with the fact this is the real world, that I'm limited in what I can do, that I've forgotten the first rule of playing in a campaign—never do what the GM expects."

"The GM?" Alexa shot a look over at Lily.

"Not Lily," I said, shaking my head. "It's more of an analogy. We've been tackling these problems head on, instead of thinking creatively, like the drug."

"Go on." Alexa leaned on the counter, the hiss and burble of the coffee pot punctuating her words.

"We went and bothered the street-level gang who's distributing the drug, but what was our plan afterward? Beat them up? How long do you think it'd take before the drugs were on the street? And really, were we going to beat up a dozen gangsters and God knows how many peons?" I shook my head. "Our job is to figure out the increase in the drugs. So why not move up the chain? If we can figure out who is making it—or bringing it into town—it'd be much more effective."

"Isn't that what we had planned?" Alexa asked simply, shaking her head. "We wanted a sample and an idea of what's happening. And what makes you think they aren't making it themselves?"

"Oh." I paused, realizing she had actually thought it through a little more than I had. Oops… "But yeah, let's stop bothering the Skulls. Let's find out who's making it!"

"That's a great idea," Alexa said simply, only the barest traces of sarcasm in her voice. "How?"

"Ummm…" I paused, gathering my flitting thoughts. "Well, we should probably talk to Andy again and see if we can get some samples like we had planned at the start. Then I can look into using a Link spell. If I time it right, and they're producing or distributing it, the largest quantities should be the easiest area to locate. Might need to adjust the spell a bit…" I trailed off, my mind swirling as I played with the idea of linking it to a map or something. Or perhaps enchanting a map and then linking the sample to it so that areas with a significant magical signature would show up.

Alexa nodded slowly. "I can do that. Now that you've introduced me, it shouldn't be difficult."

"Great," I said, snapping back to reality. "The mushrooms, we should stop trying to do it ourselves. There's no rule saying we must. I bet if I spend a few hours enchanting, I can create a simple Linked spell on a compass with a low charge on it. If we hire a few people and give them that, it'll solve our problem."

"Except we don't have the money for it," Alexa pointed out.

"But the spotted Wynn mushrooms always grow with normal Wynns, right? So if we let them keep all the Wynn mushrooms, we can just keep the spotted Wynn for ourselves," I said.

"What's to stop them from shortchanging us?" Alexa asked, and I paused to consider it. There was a chance of that for sure. It wasn't as if we could watch them.

"Nothing," I said. "But I won't charge up the compasses too much, so if we think they're cheating us, we just won't charge theirs again."

"And you can build this?" Alexa asked softly, glancing sideways at the small pile of still-unpacked crafting material. Thus far, a lot of my work has been on blocks of wood because, well, I'm still learning.

"Sure," I said, nodding. "It shouldn't be too different from the wards."

"Shouldn't."

I shrugged, then brightened, looking at Lily. "Can you tell me what my chances are?"

Lily looked up from her computers for a second, pursing her lips. She stared between the pair of us before she sighed and nodded. "You can do it, given enough time. The knowledge is all there, and with Caleb's help, it shouldn't be a problem."

"How long?" Alexa asked softly, obviously concerned by that factor.

"A day or two?" I replied, semi-confidently. It wasn't as if I'd ever done this before. At her grimace, I added. "It's still faster than us tramping around ourselves, and we can always look to do that later if we can't finish this up."

"Fine." Alexa nodded. "I'm assuming you're going to need some compasses? Anything else?"

I nodded happily, reaching for the piece of paper where I had scribbled everything I thought I'd need. "I might have more after I speak with Caleb."

"Of course," Alexa said as she poured our cups of coffee, expertly mixing the drink in our preferred ratios. Alexa took hers black, but mine was filled with milk and sugar in large quantities. Lily took hers with milk but no sugar, though the cup itself was left on the counter, forcing the jinn to stand to retrieve her drink. Even if she didn't technically have a real physical body, sitting in the same spot for hours couldn't be good for her. "Any thoughts on the last quest?"

"That…" I frowned, shaking my head. "We'll need to do some research on it. If this was really a game, the developer would have some easily exploitable flaw. Maybe we could have blackmailed him or when we set a watch, we could catch him bribing the inspectors. If it was a game, the abbess would have a number of simple quests that would tell us what to kill, find, or destroy to fix the ritual."

"But this isn't a game," Alexa said. "All right then. I don't have training this morning, so I'll pick up your supplies and some samples—if Andy has any—of the drug. I'll drop it off here and then I'll do some research on Weeks. Perhaps I can find a handle on him. You get enchanting after classes."

"Sounds like a plan," I said. Once that was settled, we ate breakfast—toast and jam today—before heading out. After all, we all had things to do.

Chapter 7

"So these new quests are sufficient motivation, are they?" Caleb asked with a smirk after I had explained what I wanted from him when I arrived for class.

"Can you help me?"

"Of course I can." Caleb tapped his lips. "It is a divergence from our training plan, however. We are trying to shore up your incompetencies, not expand on them."

"It's a spell I already know!" I gritted my teeth slightly as I tried to make Caleb deviate from his planned lesson. "It's just a way to work it better."

"A spell that, at your level of knowledge, you should not be able to cast. At least until another year," Caleb said with a sniff. "Perhaps you should just consider not placing yourself in a situation where you might need to dual cast your spells."

I growled. "Oh, come on. If you help me on this, it'll go a lot faster than me trying to work it out myself. It's just the calculations to create a semi-complete sphere are killing me."

"As they should," Caleb said with another sniff. "Stretching your container in a semi-complete sphere to cover oneself is considered a significant milestone. The requirements to adjust the size, volume, and positioning of such a defense is one of the testing principles of an apprentice mage. Obviously, the thickness and dimensions of your container will alter as different amounts of mana are input. In addition, you'll need to ensure the mana flows to each portion of the container at the same rate to ensure consistent durability."

"Yeah, I got that, but the equation itself shouldn't be that different. But whenever I use the one you provided, it doesn't really work that well. It leaks mana like a sieve," I said, trying a new tactic.

"Your control must have improved if it is only leaking that badly," Caleb said with a curl of his lip. "A protective shield that covers both your front and back equally requires a different equation. While it is possible to create the initial shield container using the current formula you have, there are significantly more mana-appropriate equations. Furthermore, due to the nature of the defense, you cannot use the basic Force Shield spell formula for redirecting energy. Not even the one altered by your Lily would work. If you do, the shield itself will be too brittle."

"Really?" I frowned, tilting my head. "But isn't the formula for mana use the same? After all, the initial spell takes into consideration multiple impacts."

"It does, but you are forgetting that you are—at your level—only directing mana from a single point. Here." Caleb walked to the blackboard he kept in this office and quickly sketched the formula and then highlighted points on it. "You see? This portion…"

I kept silent, happy to keep listening. For all that Caleb disliked me, Lily, and the situation we were in, he was also a born teacher. He enjoyed talking about magic and dispensing knowledge—or perhaps lording over his greater knowledge on another. In either case, he was always intent on making sure I understood why my current thought was inefficient or just plain wrong.

"Are you listening?"

"Yes. But why is the coefficient…" I focused back on the board, making a mental note to divert him later when I needed an answer on the enchantments. Springing my need for further education on rituals was probably a bad idea, at least right now. Step by step, I would get the knowledge I needed.

***

Hours later, I walked out of the office building feeling the need for fresh air and quiet. A series of deep breaths helped calm my roiling mind, the constant high-level discussion of concepts that I barely grasped settling down as I walked back. Classes with Caleb reminded me how strange the concepts that Lily stuffed into my brain were. Initial spell casting and spell usage were at the most basic, simple form. Yet, if I dug and studied the spell itself, other concepts would slowly peel apart, making an appearance in my mind as I made use of the spell. In time, I could even modify those spell formulas to create my own version of traditional spells.

It contrasted with the way Caleb taught, in his meticulous and detailed manner, the various theories, concepts, and formulas that made up modern magic. His teaching style forced me to truly understand the relationship between each formula, each concept before I moved to the next. And, like in the last few hours, when his lessons butted against the implanted knowledge provided by Lily, it managed to drag concepts that I had yet to fully grasp to the forefront for my use. As it stood, without the implanted knowledge by Lily, it would have taken months for me to learn to cast my new, modified Force Shield. Now, I could do so in a fraction of a second.

Even if my synchronicity sucked.

By the time I got back home, unmolested, Alexa had come and gone. A series of bags had been set aside with the various pieces of equipment I had requested. A few cheap compasses purchased from the local dollar store, spools of copper and steel wire, and various pieces of tape and string were in a box. She even included the various markers I had requested, which made me happy. A few minutes later, I had that and my "enchanting tools" spread out in the middle of the living room as my first workplace area. I studied everything I had laid out, most of which were various hobby craft scalpels, knives, and chisels taken from my original tool set and what the initiate had purchased for me.

The second workplace was much smaller and temporarily set up on the island that separated the kitchen from the rest of the house. There, I had the three small Ziploc bags of goldish-yellow dust set aside on a white plate next to a laminated city map. I figured I'd get to that project later if I could figure out this one first.

Sitting at my first workstation, I ran my hands over the pieces while I worked through the spell formula in my mind. Enchanting was, technically, simple. All I had to do was Link the spotted Wynn mushroom to the compass which then needed to be linked to a power source. In this case, the power source was mana itself. Before, with my wood blocks, I chucked the mana directly into the block itself via a holding rune. I could do the same here, but the poor plastic pieces were elementally stable. I'd be spending more mana inputting the mana into the plastic than storing it, and the extraction process would be just as bad.

No. Storage would have to be done either via something like wood, which stored mana easily but could not hold much in general, or metal, which could hold significant quantities of mana but might not necessarily be easy to store or extract. Metal had an incredibly high resistance to alteration. My other option, which was where the experimenting part came in, was looking for something less traditional. I chuckled softly to myself, tapping a pack of AAA batteries.

"Baking sheet," Lily intoned before I began.

"What?"

"Put a baking sheet down. And maybe grab a pot too," Lily said. "If you remember your last experiment…"

"Oh," I said, pausing. Right. I'd melted more than one pot and wrecked the bathroom in our old place because of my experiments. Sadly, we didn't have much of a backyard, or else I'd use that. Or maybe not. Making plain blocks of wood ignite was probably going to get difficult to explain after a while.

Once I was set up again, I picked up a battery and rolled it around the palm of my hand as I considered what I wanted to try. The first attempt was to run my mana through it, gently. No attempt at storage, no carving of runes. If passage through the battery was easy, it should work. After drawing a deep breath, I focused and emitted a trickle of mana from my hand into the battery, holding it between the tips of my fingers and thumb. Just in case.

I smiled slightly when I noticed how much easier pushing mana through the battery was than I would have expected. In fact, what I was doing had nothing to do with the contents of the battery itself—except at the most basic level. What I was betting on was using the concept of batteries.

Magic was a little mysticism and a little science. Our perceptions altered how magic was used and affected just as much as the hard "rules" of magic. Like a ritual, the use of common concepts allowed magic to flow easier. Since everyone knew you could pass energy through batteries easily and store energy in them, I had theorized using an actual battery would make the entire thing easier.

"Owww!" I shouted, dropping the suddenly melting and overheated battery onto the baking sheet while waving my burned hand around. I winced slightly, sucking on my thumb as I cast a Heal spell on myself, then waited for my body to deal with the light burns. "What the hell?"

I stared at the battery that continued to bubble, my Mage Sight showing the last traces of the mana I had input interacting with the normal chemical processes that made up the battery. I frowned, reaching out to tap against the table in thought, and received a nasty shock when I accidentally touched the baking sheet.

"Owww!"

"Shhhhh!" Lily hissed at me, not even looking up from her laptops.

I growled slightly, waving my hand to shake the pins and needles away. It wasn't a horrible shock, and the Heal spell I was channeling through my body was already healing it, but it had been painful—like receiving a shock of static electricity, except ten times as bad.

"Now what happened?" I asked with a frown. Everything had been going well. I hadn't even noticed what changed, caught up in my success as I had been. If it had been a major change, I was sure I'd have noticed it. So whatever it was, it had been minor—or something that had been happening all along. As the pain in my hands faded, I grimaced and stared at the pack of batteries. There really was no way to know without testing it further.

Four batteries and a pair of slightly scorched fingers later, I sighed and leaned back in my chair. When I inhaled again, the acrid odor of melted metal and plastic from the batteries assaulted my nose. Wincing, I took the time to clean the mess, scraping the batteries off the baking sheet into the garbage bin outside before I returned.

The problem was the fact that mundane chemistry was interacting with magic—with the mana—and basically kickstarted and ran the chemical processes so long as mana was flowing through the battery. Since I hadn't kept any formed storage runes, after I took my hands away, the mana itself slowly dispersed and returned the amount within the battery to its normal, ambient amount. During the process, the battery would continue to run, overheating itself.

Now that I knew what was happening, the question was if I could do something about it. Thus far, I was leaning toward no. Even the trickle of mana I was using was overheating the battery, forcing the chemical reaction within it to work overtime. If it wasn't for the fact that my mana flow insulated me from the actual flow of electricity when I was channeling, I'd have probably noticed the issue earlier. Unfortunately, even if I managed to stop the battery from overheating now by controlling how much mana I stored in the battery, there was no guarantee I could do the same when it was linked to the compass.

So my problem was threefold. Firstly, I had to keep the battery from overheating. Secondly, I had to ensure the battery could store the mana in a decent volume. Lastly, I needed to regulate the amount of draw from the battery so that the runes I used to regulate the battery were not overridden. Easy peasy, lemon squeezy.

Pushing aside the baking sheet and batteries for the moment, I pulled the notebook close and started sketching the runes and the interactions I figured I'd need. It was a habit I had learned from Caleb, working through the necessary enchantment and links on paper before I began the laborious process of actually carving the runes and enchantments. Alongside the runes, I also scribbled down the various spell formulas I was considering, using the shorthand that had been stuck in my brain by Lily for this purpose.

The fact that I was beginning to link multiple spells—each of which were their own rune or set of runes—meant the actual process was beginning to get complicated. While there were no set designs that were correct, the process of drawing and elaborating the runes on paper firmed up the spell formula and their relations in my mind, which made the actual carving and enchanting process smoother.

"Eat," Lily said softly, setting a bowl of instant noodles next to me. I frowned slightly, noting the chunks of meat and the pitiful strings of vegetables that had been added while Lily sauntered back to her chair, a much larger bowl in her hands.

"Thanks," I said slowly, standing and stretching as my back proceeded to inform me how long I had been hunched over. I winced, swinging my arms around and doing some general calisthenics as my body adjusted before I dove into my food. Ah, instant noodles. I missed thee.

"How is it coming along?" Lily enquired, seated with a leg cocked up on a table with her bowl of noodles in her hands.

"Pretty decent," I said simply. "I have the spell formula worked out. Even tested it out…" I gestured to the burnt remnants of the paper in the pot. "The compass Link and draw aspect seems to work, at least from what I saw." Before it burst into flames from exceeding the paper's ability to withstand the mana I had flooded through it. "Now, I just have to see if I can make the battery. Worst-case scenario, I'll enchant a block of metal and use it as the battery."

"You're going to superglue a hunk of iron to the compass?" Lily asked, eyes glittering with amusement.

"If it works…"

"It's ugly."

"Not sure that's the saying," I said, which made Lily snort with amusement again, but she dropped the topic. After all, she could comment but not advise. At least, not directly.

Next was the development of the batteries themselves. Rather than enchanting each one individually with the required spells, I decided instead to save myself the trouble by creating a mana charger for the battery. By enchanting a block of wood to firstly lower the temperature of the batteries placed within and secondly control the amount of energy drawn, I could skip any complicated enchantments on the batteries themselves. I still had to enchant the batteries to store mana, but that was a significantly simpler process.

With a nod, I grabbed the soldering iron and grabbed the nearest battery. Best to get started then. As it was, soldering the design was going to be painful. It'd been ages since I actually picked up my soldering kit, and it really was not like riding a bicycle. Grimacing at the ugly beads I ended up leaving on the battery, I slowly reached out with my senses to check if the enchantment had worked.

Storage Ward Created (17% Efficiency)

"Thanks, Lily," I called out, grateful for her aid. Even if I could sense it myself, the displayed data was significantly more effective and efficient. I liked numbers, and this one at least gave me an idea of how well I'd done with my cobbled-together spell.

Now, I just had to carve out a block of wood to fit the battery, make sure the carvings for the Alter Temperature and Channel Wards were correct and then Link it to the compass. Simple.

***

"Goddamn it!" I snarled, sucking on my bleeding palm. I hated carving. I really, really hated carving. Glaring at the block, I drew a deep breath and channeled my Heal spell once again. Once again, I was grateful we had hardwood floors rather than carpet. Otherwise, we'd have lost another damage deposit from the amount of blood I'd lost. Amazing how even a relatively light cut could bleed.

"No luck?" Alexa asked when she walked down the stairs from her room, clad in a new set of clothing after her bath.

"None so far," I said with a grimace, glancing at the duo of carved and discarded blocks by the side. The first had been carved perfectly—and then I realized it could not work because I had no way of storing mana inside the block itself, making the refrigeration option impossible to work. I'd then attempted to modify it, to begin the moment I started channeling mana to store in the battery, but that had just ended up with a melted battery as the Alter Temperature rune took too long to get working.

My second attempt had not gone much better. After adding a storage rune on my mana charger, I had charged it with mana directly. That had worked well, but the reduction in temperature achieved by the initial spell had been significantly less than I had expected. After returning to the drawing board and figuring out how to adjust the spell by focusing the Alter Temperature container to just the battery location, I was working on my third block.

"Are you at least making progress?" Alexa asked as she leaned over my chair. I glanced at the blonde again, distractedly noting she'd gone for a sweater-and-sweatpants combo.

"Some. It'll get done by tomorrow at the latest," I said firmly. In fact, I did not mention I could have finished it today if I wasn't actually experimenting on these mana chargers. While it was important for my own development, we were on a timetable. "How'd you do?"

"Not much better. I spent most of the day watching his office. It's an office."

"And he didn't notice?"

"He works out of the second floor of a retail space. And there's a hairdresser who had a spot open," Alexa said simply, touching her hair hesitantly.

I turned my head and regarded her new do, a pixie-style haircut that included some very modest highlights.

"So…"

"Ummm… it's nice?" I said slowly, uncertain of what she was looking for. It was a haircut.

"It is, isn't it?" Alexa said with a smile and then straightened. "I'll make dinner."

"Great." I stared as the blonde initiate bounced off into the kitchen and then I exhaled in relief as my brain came out of enchanting fog. I barely escaped the jaws of death on that one.

Well, it did help it was nice.

Chapter 8

"You're mine," I growled softly at the wooden block the next morning. Alexa had left to see if she could dig up more information about the property developer who was interested in the orphanage while I had promised to get this enchanting job done. To put even more pressure on me, Alexa had promised to arrange the appointments with our scavengers for later tonight, which meant I needed this done.

After spending the night sleeping like the dead, I had woken up with a clearer idea of what I needed to do. Perhaps the lack of sleep the night before coupled with my experiences yesterday had clarified things, but staring at my previous day's work, I saw numerous flaws in the enchantment—over and above my poor crafting skills of course. After lacing my fingers together, I stretched them out before I bent over the wooden block, chisel in hand.

A few hours later, I finally had a working prototype. Like all prototypes, it was ugly as sin, barely functioning, and inefficient, but it proved the concept. After some tweaking and dropping nearly my entire mana pool into the charger, I was able to link it with the compass directly for the initial test. Using a simple metal clip, I made sure to link the pair together, allowing the compass to point toward the nearest spotted Wynn mushroom.

The entire contraption was, as mentioned, ugly. A plain wooden block was glued to a plastic compass which had a small spot dug out for the mushroom sample in it. The sample itself was held in place via sticky tape, which allowed me to theoretically switch out the linked material at any time. The block had numerous, badly done carvings of the enchantment runes on it while the compass had a series of gouged out runes on it as well. In the wooden block, a portion of it had been carved out such that the batteries may be inserted and linked to the entire contraption. Overall, it looked like something a twelve-year-old kid would make in a bad eighties' kids' movie. It was, in other words, perfect.

Modular Compass and Mana Battery Integrated Gadget
Efficiency: 21%
Duration: 4 hours and 5 minutes using current stored battery charge

I smiled slightly, staring at the information. Perfect. The batteries, as I figured, could hold the charge much longer than a simple block of wood or metal. If I had tried to do the same with the materials I had, I could at best store a total of two hours of work. Now, I had nearly doubled the storage capacity. If I carved a second storage channel for a second battery, I could even potentially double the lifespan. Or, and this was the genius of the concept, just hand them pre-charged mana batteries to swap out. After all, it was in the initial charging and discharging phase the batteries were dangerous. Storing them, thus far, seemed to perfectly safe.

Of course, I had to add thus far. With a grimace, I made a note to store these batteries in a cooking pot somewhere non-flammable. Just in case.

"Don't you need the initial charger?" Lily's voice woke me from my self-satisfied stupor. I still hadn't built the initial charger that regulated the batteries while I was charging them, ensuring they didn't overheat. Once it was built, I could just add mana directly to the charger, pre-charging a slew of mana batteries. On top of that, I also needed to build at least a couple more of these blocks since Alexa had booked three scavengers to arrive.

I winced slightly, flexing stiff fingers, and I stared at the next block of wood. Right. No rest for the talented.

***

Reworking the enchantments for the next couple blocks was significantly easier. Of course, I grumpily wished this was a game—or at least had easy crafting options like most games. Thankfully, everything I was doing currently required minimal actual skill. Etching, carving, and soldering were all within my wheelhouse. Blacksmithing, glassblowing, and tanning were crafting areas I was going to ignore for now. I certainly did not have the time to spend learning how to forge a sword properly, no matter how cool it would be to have a magical sword.

After I completed all three blocks, I turned to my second enchanting station. This one was significantly simpler in theory. I picked up a bottle of ink and began the process of lightly imbuing it with my mana. I wanted the ink to be mana imbued because what I wanted to do next was drawn from a magic trick I recalled seeing before.

First, Link the Leprechaun's Foot to the laminated map. Then, Link the map to the city… or the concept of the city. That, of course, was more difficult. Thankfully, as a representation of the city itself, the map did not require significant amounts of mana to achieve the link. Next, Link the drug to the ink and to the map at the same time. Then I would have to cast a Track spell while Linking that spell to the ink which was linked to the map. Lastly, if my theory was correct, all I had to do was pour the ink on the map.

Of course, creating so many Links at the same time was going to be difficult. I needed a very high level of synchronicity for this to work on each Link as their efficacy would break down along the chain. It was sort of like linking numerous pieces of wire together for electricity—you always had a loss of current the more you added. As such, while the actual theory was simple, doing it was less than simple. What the level of synchronicity I needed was… well, that was what experimentation was for.

Worse, Caleb had indicated doing something like this was considered a "simple" task for any "real" mage apprentice. Of course, at times I was uncertain how much to believe him. The mage was not above exaggerating to make me work harder.

"Ninth time's the charm," I muttered, staring at the pieces of equipment strewn around me. I took a moment to feel my mana level and sighed. Right, time for a break first. I needed at least two-thirds of my pool to do this safely, and I was just under half right now.

"Great! I'm hungry," Lily called.

"Make it yourself," I grumbled.

"But you're in the kitchen…" Lily did have a point.

"Pizza?"

"Have I ever said no?"

I dug into our freezer and quickly pulled out a frozen pizza, then turned the oven on to preheat it. Then, spotting the time, I decided to grab a second pizza, knowing Alexa would be back. Ah, the convenience of ready-made meals. I prepped the pizza sheets, pulled them aside and then took a break to hit the washroom. By the time I was done, the oven was ready and so was my mana pool.

Standing over my equipment, I drew a deep breath, forcing myself to focus again as I began the process once more. First, drug to map. Then map to the concept of the city. Mana rushed out of me in a torrent. Once the connection was made, I continued the process, carefully "sewing" the Links between each piece. In the end, I stared at the 41 percent Link efficiency I had and nodded to myself. Good enough. All that practice and previous attempts seemed to have done some good.

After drawing a deep breath, I cast a Track spell, holding the Linked aspects together through the process. My head throbbed, but I pushed it aside, the numerous portions of the spell pressing against my mind. I chanted the words of the spell softly, forced to rely only on the oral components to keep the spell together.

The ink dribbled from the bottle slowly as I poured, my mana seeming to fall with the ink itself. I gritted my teeth as a headache began to form beneath my eyebrows, but I pushed forward. I was not going to stop. As the ink fell, it began to squirm on the map, flowing to pool in larger and smaller concentrations in different places. Some of the concentrations were no more than dots, others a quarter of the size of a dime. The smallest dots even shifted slightly, most on roads of some sort when they did. When the last of the ink fell, I exhaled and put the bottle aside and grabbed my phone. A few quick photos later, I finally released the spell.

Thankfully, the ink did not run much even when it was no longer magically bound to specific locations, allowing me to take a few further photographs just in case. I smiled slightly, staring at the result. Not a bad result, for a mostly theoretical and impromptu spell. Even if it was cobbled together from the basics of other, more-established spells.

"That our map?" Alexa asked, making me jump and let out a very manly shriek.

"Oooh…" The face of a thin, angular creature in grey—who stood nearly eight feet tall—twitched, and it rubbed furiously at its ear. "Do you sing soprano?"

"That… you… When did you get here?" I asked in a low, masculine tone.

"About five minutes ago," the thin man said. "That was a great show."

"It was impressive. So those are where we need to go?" Alexa asked again, and this time, I answered her affirmatively. "Great. Corey here has agreed to your proposal."

"My… Ah! For the mushrooms," I said and grinned. I almost ran to the table, proudly showing them my latest invention. However, rather than looking impressed like with the map, the pair instead looked somewhat confused. "What?"

"It's a bit ugly," Corey finally said.

"It's effective!" I growled, shoving the compass-and-block getup at him. "Once the battery runs out, you just need to come back and swap the batteries for new ones that we'll have here. And hand us the spotted Wynn you've collected."

Corey turned the compass hand over hand, staring at the enchanted piece of equipment before he finally opened his mouth to speak slowly. "And it'll point the way to the nearest spotted Wynn?"

"Pretty much." I nodded. "Nearest and biggest. The Link spell looks for the strongest connection, so if there's a mushroom or a set of mushrooms, it'll more likely lead you there than toward a single one."

"Amazing. And it looks like you can do it for any item?" Corey asked, touching the tape.

"Sort of," I said with a shrug. "It's a bit more complicated than just choosing what I want, but yes."

"That's incredible." Corey licked his lips, a glint of avarice in his eyes. I frowned, leaning forward and tapping the table to get his attention.

"Two things. This doesn't go any further. And secondly, remember, the batteries are only chargeable by me. Unless you want to contact a real mage and ask him to play with that." I gestured at the mashed-together piece of equipment. I watched Corey's face change as he considered the fact. Most mages were arrogant asses. Asking them to work with a piece of equipment like the one he held would be demeaning for them, and no one wanted to annoy a mage.

"It's cool, man. It's cool. I was just thinking," Corey said with a grin. "I'm going to go then…"

"Go ahead," I said, waving him off. Once the thin man had gone, I raised an eyebrow at Alexa. "I thought there were others?"

"So did I," Alexa said grumpily and glanced at the clock. I guess even in the supernatural world, flakes were a thing. Changing the subject, Alexa pointed at the map. "I'm assuming the biggest ink blot is where we're going next?"

"Yes. Slowly and carefully," I said. If we were going to act against a distributor or producer, we definitely needed to play this smarter than the last time.

Alexa nodded back at me firmly, obviously thinking the same thing.

Chapter 9

"Are you sure we're in the right place?" Alexa asked softly for the second time as we drove through the tree-lined residential neighborhood. Each detached house adjoined the next in their suburban sameness, though occasional reconstruction broke the monotony of the two-story, cookie-cutter homes with their attached garages and perfectly manicured lawns.

"That's what the map says," I muttered. I had my hand on the drug as well while we slowly and carefully drove down the streets. Not too slow, just slow enough to look like a careful, civic-minded driver not wishing to run over careless children.

"This doesn't look like a drug lab…" Alexa shook her head. "Or a place to store illegal drugs."

"Well, it's not exactly illegal," I said, tapping the cyan chemical compound in its Ziploc baggie in my hand. "It's not like police are knocking down doors over Leprechaun's Foot."

Alexa pursed her lips but nodded after a moment. That was true enough. This was a supernatural drug, with supernatural enhancements. Production and effect on individuals, even at the largest level, most likely would never look like more than a blip to the federal government. As it stood, there were many more dangerous drugs to deal with affecting the mundane population. Heck, modern chemical testing probably wouldn't even see anything wrong with it.

"So…" Alexa said leadingly.

"Three doors down," I said quietly after a moment. "I'm sure it's that one."

"Are you seeing anything?"

"Noooo," I said, squinting. "Actually, yes. There's a distortion in the air around the building, like a heatwave. Reminds me of the way Caleb looks when he's channeling…" I paused to consider for a moment. "But this is a lot more stable. So less like channeling and more like it's a fixed point of distortion."

"What would do that?" Alexa asked softly, her foot barely shifting when we passed the house. Both of us stared at the simple, cream-colored building with light-brown highlights and a simple brick rooftop infested with solar panels. I wondered if the panels were to hide their usage of electricity… if they needed to use electricity. Or perhaps they were environmentalists? Supernatural, gangster environmentalists. A mind-boggling thought. Other than that, with the white curtains drawn, we could see nothing of note. Even the garage was closed, with no vehicles to give further hints.

"Looks normal," I muttered.

"Other than the magical disturbance?" Alexa said sarcastically, turning her attention back toward the road. "I think if we park up that hill, we could get a view of this house." Alexa jerked her head, indicating the hill directly in front of us.

"Sounds good," I said and started looking up directions on my phone. "And yes, normal except the magical disturbance. Pretty sure it's the Leprechaun's Foot."

"I really hate that name."

***

Thirty minutes and two wrong turns later, we found ourselves at a small, gravel shoulder on the hill. Alexa, of course, had a pair of binoculars in the car, which we took turns using to watch the house. Unfortunately, watching the building from a distance currently provided us very little information.

"How'd the investigation on the developer go?" I asked to break the silence.

"Slow." Alexa sighed. "But I'm nearly a hundred percent certain he's a blind."

"Blind?"

"Ah. You call them mundanes. Norms. Muggles," Alexa said.

"Isn't that copyrighted?"

"Who's going to tell her?" Alexa smirked, and I chuckled softly.

"So he's just being an ass?"

"Pretty much," Alexa said with a sigh. "I dug into the fines and notices the orphanage was given. They aren't exactly wrong. The rules and regulations the orphanage is in breach of are just updates on existing code. Normally, they wouldn't be applied till the orphanage needed to apply for a new license or did some work, but—"

"But it doesn't mean they aren't necessary," I said slowly. "And because it's an orphanage, it'd be harder to say: 'We don't need to bring these things up to code.'"

"Exactly," Alexa said. "I don't really know what we can do there. I've contacted a few lawyers, hopefully some of them will help us slow down the fines. That might be the best we can do about the developer. Unless we can find some dirt on him, and beyond a penchant for bribing bureaucrats to do their job, I've got nothing."

"Which leaves the fact that the contractors won't go back into the storage room because it's haunted, and you've got a series of failing rituals to contend with."

"Yes."

"Fine. That's next on the list then," I said with some resignation. Now, I really wished this was more like one of my stupid, linear computer RPGs. Most of those games involved running around and beating up the latest beholder or messing with the evil warlock. They didn't involve figuring out how to thwart the evil merchant from buying the orphanage that was annoying him. Or, well, it did, but I'd just blast him with a fireball in a game and call it a day.

Somehow, premeditated murder did not seem as fun in reality. With that sobering thought, I fell silent as the pair of us watched the house. Perhaps some brilliant idea would occur to us later.

***

"I should have brought a book," I muttered a few hours later.

"We're supposed to be watching the building," Alexa said softly.

"For what?" I asked. "I mean, they joke about how stakeouts suck, but really…"

"They do?"

"They really do." I shifted in my seat to settle my back. "I mean, what are we supposed to be doing here? Watching a house to see what? Who comes out and drives away? I swear, I could find a spell for this…"

"Mages and your spells," Alexa said.

"Come on, you can't say you're enjoying this," I said.

"Enjoy? No. But it is necessary. This is how you gather information."

"Maybe this is how you gather information, but I'm a mage," I said firmly. "I'm going to figure out a smarter way of doing this."

"Go ahead," Alexa said, getting impatient.

I nodded firmly and then fell silent, going over my character sheet and spell list to start.

Class: Mage
Level 22 (29% Experience)
Known Spells: Light Sphere, Force Spear, Force Shield, Force Fingers, Alter Temperature, Gong, Gust, Heal, Healing Ward, Link, Track, Fix, Ward, Glamour, Illusion, Summon, Iceball, Fireball, Scry

I chuckled when I noted I'd leveled up. I vaguely recalled there had been that notification while I had been working on the map yesterday, but I'd been a touch busy. And obsessed. I would admit to a little obsession. Still, as I eyed the spells, I blinked at the latest. Huh…

And huh.

I half-closed my eyes and concentrated, pulling at the spell in my mind. It came to the forefront of my thoughts with a flash, a piece of knowledge that had always been there just waiting for me to focus on it. I'd considered it a coincidence that the spell I desperately needed was right here, at my fingertips—except for the fact that, of course, I had a GM who was watching over all this. I'd bet Lily had made sure to gift this spell to me because she knew what I'd need.

Scry. A simple enough spell at the lowest levels of mastery. It actually was a compound spell like Fireball or Iceball. It built upon known spells, streamlined via specific formulas that made the spell more powerful but more restrictive. In this case, the Scry spell was built upon Link, Track, and

Illusion. The Track portion basically guided the spell to the location you were looking for, Link linked the spell component you were using to an appropriate target within the location, and Illusion displayed the location. It was a triple-compound spell, one that was no more difficult to do than creating my map but more strenuous since I wasn't just linking to a conceptual city but an actual space. As such, the requirements for refinement and fidelity were higher.

Still, the Scry spell was exactly what I needed. Firstly though, I'd need a linking material—an appropriate medium. The most common items were mirrors, crystal balls, and bowls of water. Each would link to a mirror, glass, or water in the surroundings, which meant none were particularly better than the other in general. Though, from the knowledge forced into me, some were clearer than others.

Thankfully, I was in a car, so finding a mirror was a simple matter. Alexa shot me a glance when I adjusted the rearview mirror, but I decided to ignore her for the moment. Since this was the first time I was casting the spell, I figured I'd better test it out before discussing it. Wouldn't want it to fizzle out.

My fingers moved, and my mouth chanted as my mind ran through the newly provided spell formula and mana flowed through my body and out my fingertips. My perception lurched as mana flowed out of me, carrying me out of my body as the spell nearly completed. The sudden change—even if I knew subconsciously that it was about to happen—was too much for me and the spell broke, shattering around me and sending shards of free-floating mana running through me. I grunted, shuddering, and closed my eyes.

Damn it. I hadn't expected to fail at the start.

"Henry?"

"Testing a new spell," I said once I got my breath back. I leaned back for a few moments, letting my body slowly calm and the pain subside while I went over the details of the spell again. This time, I wouldn't let myself fail. Even if the out-of-body experience was weird.

Once again, I cast the spell and felt my mana leave me. I exhaled slowly and closed my eyes, feeling the lurch once more as my senses left my body. This time though, I was prepared for the feeling and continued to chant the spell, guiding my temporary self to the location. It really was just my senses, and even then, it wasn't the entirety of them. It was a vertigo-inducing moment, and by the time I had mostly adjusted, I'd covered the hundreds of yards to the house. I even overshot my location and had to retreat, adjusting the spell formulas of the Scry spell on the fly.

Sensing in this state was at the most crude, rudimentary stage. I could not see, hear, or smell anything, but I could sense where various mirrors and objects close enough to a reflective surface were. I could even sense, to an extent, the level of appropriateness for me to Link my spell. At a higher level, I would even be able to Link multiple items at the same time, but for now, I picked the highest appropriate Link item and sent my body back to the car. A fraction of a second later, I opened my eyes.

Scry Cast
Synchronicity 31%
Link 78%

Blinking away the notification, I turned to look at the rearview mirror, which now showed a new reflection. My smile held for a fraction of a second before I huffed out loud, while Alexa sniggered slightly at the image shown.

Right. Highest appropriateness meant another mirror. And where were most mirrors? In bedrooms and bathrooms. Staring at the blurry, white-tiled interior of an empty bathroom, I huffed in annoyance again. Well, at least the spell worked.

***

"Is this how it's normally done?" Alexa asked a half hour later after I'd cast and recast Scry, trying to find a good location to spy on those within. Thus far, we'd peeked into empty bedrooms, an empty closet, and an empty kitchen. Right now though, I had to wait for my mana to regenerate.

"No," I said, shaking my head as I prodded the information in my mind. "There are ways to lock onto multiple surfaces, then complete the spell. Then it's just a matter of flicking through them till you find the appropriate location."

"Why aren't you doing that?"

"Beginner here, remember? I'm having a hard enough time locking down a single location at this distance, never mind multiple. And the amount of mana required increases too, as well as the complexity of the actual spell formula." I shook my head at the thought. "Give me a bit, and I'll be able to lock down two, but for now, one and done is where we're at."

"Huh," Alexa said simply and then leaned back in her chair. A moment later, she leaned forward and grabbed her binoculars, staring ahead.

"What?" I frowned, looking at the house. It did not take me long to realize what had attracted Alexa's attention. A minivan had driven up. Unfortunately, it was one of those multi-door white minivans beloved by housewives, soccer moms, and large families everywhere. In other words, utterly useless at this distance for providing additional information. A short while later, it entered the newly opened garage.

"Can you…?"

"Already on it," I said, nodding in confirmation as I started casting Scry again. It would drop me below the 10 percent bar I'd set for myself but not too far. All it meant was I'd be eating more painkillers for the next few hours. But… "Got it. One van mirror coming up."

The mirror flickered and shifted, a new image appearing. I grimaced, making a mental note to find a bigger mirror to cart around next time since this image, drawn from the side mirror, was slightly truncated to fit everything in. With a flicker of my hand, I shifted the mirror around as distorted words came through the newly formed mirror.

"What are you doing here?" A deep, husky male voice came through first, a four-pack-a-day smoker with a cold who somehow still managed to create a feeling of dread over the communicator.

"I'm here to pick up the next shipment," a high female voice answered him. For a second, there was a flash of pale skin and an orange blouse before it was gone. I frowned, shifting the image around as I attempted to see more.

"Stop…" Alexa hissed a moment before I stopped the shifting image myself. In it, we caught our first glimpse, a female in an orange, ruffled blouse with a sneer on her lips and brown hair.

"Sold out already?" The male voice spoke again. From what I could tell, he was probably standing directly behind the mirror.

"Can't keep it on the streets. My man wants at least twice our last order," the woman said and grinned. She reached into the car, her tight pants pulling firm for a second in the image when she leaned within. I had to pause to admire the sight, a low whistle coming the other man, making me think the enviable, large, and tight posterior was being admired by more than myself.

When the lady stood straight again, this time I noted a slight grin as she exited. A bulky brown envelope was held in hand, one that she tossed over. "Same price, yes?"

The other voice chuckled. "Not going to bargain?"

"Not if you keep the exclusivity."

"Wait here." A moment later, the click of a closing door was heard. In the meantime, the young lady leaned against the now-closed van door, offering us an admirable if not particularly informative view. My fingers shifted side to side as I attempted to find a better angle and got nothing.

"Is she supernatural?" Alexa asked me as we watched.

"Can't tell. It's a good illusion if she is," I said tightly while holding the connection open. Well, glamour and illusion combined. Glamours tricked the mind; illusions tricked reality. Combined, they kept supernaturals hidden—though most of their disguises were largely glamour with the smallest amounts of illusion possible to allow supernaturals to pass common recording devices. However, the young lady in our mirror looked perfectly normal, which indicated she was either using a powerful illusion spell or wasn't using one at all.

"Bah," Alexa said softly, drumming her fingers on the wheel. A few minutes later, the door opened.

"About time," the woman said, standing. For a second, she left our field of vision, rustling and crinkling the only sound reaching us. "This looks more than double."

"Just a little extra, for our favorite customer."

"Your only customer," the woman said, a hint of aggression in her voice. The speaker just grunted in reply. A few moments later, we saw her back in our field of vision again, pulling the door open to drop a couple of brown paper bags inside.

I grunted and, as the two started exchanging goodbyes, released the spell. When Alexa turned to look at me, she noticed me breathing deeply, with sweat staining my brow, and rubbing my sore temples.

"You okay?"

"Fine. Just couldn't hold it any longer," I replied. "Give me a few hours. Once my mana's back, we can Scry it again."

"Okay," Alexa said simply. After a second's consideration, she started the car.

"I can't Track her…" I said, squinting at the house.

"I know. I was thinking we hadn't had lunch." Alexa offered me a half smile. "With your spell, we should get you fed and then come back to look again."

"Okay." I was sure there was something off about leaving the place unwatched, but considering she was doing this in consideration of my headache, I was not going to complain. And anyway, my spell was probably going to get us more information than sitting there, watching.

***

A couple hours and one plate of curried pineapple rice later, we were back at the same hill. This time around, with nearly half the likely locations already investigated, I decided I'd check out the basement level. A part of me had considered just jumping the Scry to that floor to begin with, but going below ground level actually pulled a lot more mana than staying above it. Even though the basement was technically hollowed out, the draw on my mana was still much higher than I'd care to use to start. Thus, the earlier testing.

Unfortunately, after casting the spell, I realized the biggest problem with a spell targeted to a basement that is reliant on sight: If no one turns on the lights, all you were seeing was darkness as well.

"Nothing?"

"You tell me," I said grumpily. For a brief moment, I considered if it'd be possible to cast a Light spell within the basement. It was theoretically possible. I had the spatial coordinates and even a way to see where I was casting. However, theory ran up against reality really fast. Not only would it be incredibly draining on my limited mana, it would also potentially alert our prey of our presence.

"Next?"

"Yup." I killed the spell before moving onward.

Eventually, by process of elimination, we located our targets. They were upstairs, three individuals seated watching TV in the second floor living room. Now that we had them in view, we took our time staring at the trio. Sprawled as they were on their chairs with discarded remnants of various takeout joints and snack foods, they looked almost normal. A pair of Hispanic-looking men and a shorter, Vietnamese-looking gentleman were sprawled, idly watching the idiot box. I frowned, wanting to know which had been the speaker, but all three were silent, content to damage their minds with the drivel of afternoon TV. It was a very domestic scene if you ignored the weapons in easy reach of the three: a pair of handguns and a shotgun, with a machete also laid beside them.

"How long can you hold this?" Alexa asked softly.

"Now that it's established?" I considered, judging my mana. "Twenty minutes safely. If I meditate and focus on drawing in more mana, maybe thirty. But I'd be useless for anything—"

"Do it," Alexa said firmly. "I'll watch and take notes. At the least, I want to know who their leader is."

"All right," I said in agreement while Alexa pulled a sketchbook from her supplies within the car. She immediately started sketching while I closed my eyes and focused. My breathing deepened as I reached and opened myself at the same time, allowing the mana that surrounded us to absorb into my body even as more mana flooded out while I channeled my spell. Time lost meaning as I held the two opposing concepts in mind, focused as they were within my body.

"Time," I said softly after a while. I received a grunted agreement from Alexa, so I cut the flow of power. The spell flickered, running for a few moments more on the stored power before it wound down. As I opened my eyes, I frowned as a crunch of gravel occurred a moment later, making me turn to look at a police car rolling to a stop next to us.

"Crap," Alexa said. She quickly pursed her lips and then suddenly leaned over, grabbing my shirt by the side and pulling me close.

A moment later, I found myself lip-locked with the blonde as she held me tight. At first, I struggled, then my brain caught up with me. Why exactly was I struggling against the pretty blonde who was kissing me? Wait. Why was I even thinking about anything but how soft her lips were? As my brain finally caught up, I relaxed slightly only to tense again when a rapping occurred on the window. Almost immediately, Alexa released me and adjusted her blouse, her cheeks flushed.

"Wha—"

The rapping came again, my uttered exclamation not finishing.

"Window," Alexa said slightly breathlessly and then rolled hers down to smile demurely at the policeman. "Yes, Officer?"

"We received a report there was a vehicle parked here suspiciously," the officer said. I saw his eyes dart from my to Alexa's slightly flushed faces, a slight frown creasing his face.

"Oh… I didn't know that was illegal, sir!" Alexa exclaimed artlessly. She then paused, giving him big, innocent eyes as she continued. "It isn't, is it?"

"It's not illegal, miss. We're just checking that there's nothing suspicious going on," the officer replied. His attention shifted to the mirror propped up on the dashboard, the binoculars and then to the wooden warding blocks that spilled out of my backpack in the backseat. "What are you doing up here?"

"Bird-watching!" Alexa said, then flushed slightly and looked down, biting her lip.

"Bird-watching," the officer replied dryly. "Well, I'm a bit of an ornithologist myself. See anything interesting?"

I opened and shut it. Hell, I could barely tell the difference between a crow and a raven. But Alexa replied without hesitation. "Nothing rare. A couple of thrushes, a chestnut-backed chickadee, and a goldfinch."

The officer nodded his head along to Alexa's words but relaxed slightly. "Nice to see some young people taking an interest in the hobby."

"My uncle introduced me to it," Alexa said happily and smiled.

"Well, if you're just bird-watching, you have a nice day." The officer flashed a glance at the wooden blocks and then smiled at Alexa before he shot me a much frostier look. I gave him a weak grin which made the officer snort as he walked away. With the expanded senses I had, I heard him mutter as he walked off. "I know what bird he's watching…"

I coughed slightly, shaking my head, and then looked at Alexa who continued to provide a smiling demeanor until the officer had pulled off.

"What was the kiss about?" I asked quietly, touching my lips unconsciously after I finished speaking.

"Isn't that what they do in the movies?" Alexa shrugged. "I doubt he'd take the bird-watching excuse entirely, so I added to it. It worked, didn't it?"

"I thought you weren't good at lying," I said.

"I'm not. And I wasn't," Alexa said and pointed. "Thrush. Chickadee. Oooh, that's a northern fulmar."

I stared at the sudden burst of happiness on Alexa's face and then sighed. "You had the weirdest childhood."

"Uh huh." Alexa sniffed. "I'm just enjoying the beauty of His work."

Without a rejoinder, I shifted my gaze toward her sketchbook that she had dropped down the side of her seat, out of sight of the policeman. "Anything?"

"Just sketches. They didn't really talk much, but I'm pretty sure the Asian looker was our speaker."

"Ah…" I said with a nod. Well, at least we got something from this.

"We should keep watch for a little while more before we leave," Alexa said finally and flashed me a smile.

I nodded dumbly, staring at the blonde who seemed to have forgotten the kiss already. After a moment, I could do nothing more than push it aside. As they said, don't shit where you eat. And really, I doubted the initiate had any thoughts about me like that.

Chapter 10

Dinner that evening was Greek. I grabbed an order of moussaka and a double order of calamari for everyone to share, while Alexa went the roast lamb route and Lily did them all. Which, when I realized how much food that was, was a bit much. Sometimes I had the feeling Lily ate for the experience of eating more than for the physical need. I'd certainly never have to worry about kicking her out of the washroom—which was, perhaps, the only reason the three of us had survived in my old apartment.

"Right, so where are we?" I asked as I speared another deep-fried squiddy goodness. Wait, did leviathans exist? Or squiddy Cthulhu monsters?

Rather than directly answer me, Lily popped a notification in front of my eyes. I growled, swatting the box to make it smaller so I could eat and read. I had to smile that she had even added little notations of what we had managed.

Help Alexa Complete Her Squire Trial (Chained Quest)

This is a chained quest. You must complete the sub-quests to complete the major quest.

Sub-quests:

- *Investigate and deal with the sudden influx of Leprechaun's Foot (Investigated)*
- *Collect fifty specimens of Spotted Wynn Mushrooms (28/50 collected)*

- *Help solve the Brixton Orphanage issues (Have you really even started?)*

"One out of three ain't bad?" Alexa said, pointing at air and what I assumed to be the second quest line. With the scavenger working for us, we had that one covered. I might even have figured out a way to generate additional, ongoing income in the future if this worked out well.

"But two out of three would be better," I said. When there was no immediate reaction, I looked between the two ladies and then sighed. Obviously classic eighties' rock was not a selling point with this group. "Right, so we know where they're storing the Foot. Unfortunately, it doesn't look like they're manufacturing in the city. Otherwise, we'd probably spot it on the map."

"If you say so," Alexa said before she frowned. "But if they're not manufacturing them here…"

"How do we stop it from coming in?" I said, finishing for her. "It's all about supply and demand, but demand isn't something we can affect, so we got to cut off the supply. Makes me feel like the little Dutch boy and the dam."

Again, silence from the pair.

"You know, trying to stem the tide with a finger? It's not possible. Even if we burn all the product, they'll just send more."

Alexa slowly nodded, chewing on the meat-juice-soaked rice in thought. "But we don't need to stop it completely. Our job is just to reduce it, for the time being."

"And the orphanage?" Lily asked.

"We're stuck there too. We can't really make the fines go away..." I paused, considering. Well, I could wipe their files possibly. I was sure there was a spell for that somewhere. Potentially just a small electrical surge in the offices and it'd fix the issue. As for the paper records—

"Henry?"

"Ah, just thinking I might be able to erase the fines, but it's a temporary solution, isn't it?" I asked, and the pair nodded. Still, it was worth thinking about if we needed to buy ourselves some time. Time was the major problem. We had just over a week left, and we still had not found a solution. "But maybe we could con them."

"What do you mean?" Alexa asked, and I smiled slightly.

"Well, if they do all the retrofitting in every other location first, I can look it over and cast an illusion to make the storeroom look like it's been done. It won't be, but it should last the inspection, no?"

"But what about the contractors?" Alexa asked, looking troubled. "They'd know. And we'd be lying."

"Yeah, not sure about the contractors. Maybe we could lie to them and let them go after they're done because they won't finish the work? After all, they won't be able to articulate why they don't want to go in beyond it's a bad feeling, right?" I said.

Alexa protested. "But it's not their fault!"

"No, it's the orphanage's," I said. "Who hires blinds to work on a magical building? Also. Nope. That is not a word I want to use."

"They had a limited budget."

"Uh huh," I said. "And look where being cheap has gotten them. In fact, I'm not even sure having them work on the rest of the building is a good idea." I paused, considering the matter. "In fact, scrap the idea. Our next job is finding a supernatural and magically sensitive construction group to work on this."

"I don't think the Abbess will like that…"

I just stared at Alexa, letting her work out the issues herself. In the end, the blonde let out an angry huff. "You'll want me to speak with the abbess and the contractors, right?'

"Of course. It's your quest. Maybe they could do a workaround—fortify it magically and make it look like they've done the work mundanely or something," I said. "I'll hit class with Caleb tomorrow and then I'd like to do some research on the building itself."

"And the jackals?" Alexa asked, tapping her plate as she looked at me.

"You tell me."

At my words, Alexa's eyes tightened as she considered the matter. We both had the same information. In the end, Alexa said simply, "I'm going to get clarification. If all we need to do is put a temporary hold on the supply, it can be achieved by hitting the house. If they're looking for something more permanent..." Alexa trailed off, and I nodded.

Yeah. I didn't exactly have an answer to that one either. Then again, I didn't feel too bad. It wasn't as if governments hadn't been trying and failing to solve the drug problem for the last couple hundred years.

***

"Did you finish your project?" Caleb asked the next day when I arrived.

With a slight smile, I brought out a few of the failures and some pre-prepped blocks. Caleb raised an eyebrow, while I smiled at the master mage. "I thought you could take a look at my work. See if you had any comments."

Caleb tapped his lips in thought before he waved his hand, gesturing for me to start. Once I had the blocks and my equipment set aside—after a slight coughing fit by Caleb when I first pulled out my tools—I focused and started working. In a mere fifteen minutes, I had another modular compass and mana battery made. Thankfully, once I actually had the plans developed, it was easy enough to finish the work. I even threw in a new twist to some of the sigils, which seemed to increase the effectiveness of the enchanted equipment ever so slightly.

"Well, it's not the most elegant of equipment," Caleb said as he turned the block around in his hand. He tapped the batteries, a wry smile on his lips. "And it does rebuild the wheel with these batteries. But there are some interesting twists to the spells you've used, some of which I might even call genius." I began to grow pleased at Caleb's words before he added. "But then, you did pull them from your 'downloaded' spells, so it is no surprise." Caleb fished in his pockets and pulled out his wallet, drawing out four crisp bills before he handed them to me. "I will purchase this contraption from you."

"Really?" I said, my eyes wide.

"Of course. As I said, some of the mana formulas you have interlaced in the block is quite ingenious. It is much simpler to study the spells that your jinn has implanted in your mind through something like this"—Caleb tapped the mana compass—"than attempting to transcribe your explanations."

"Oh…" I exhaled disappointedly. It didn't stop me from taking the bills though and sliding them into my back pocket. "Well, if it was so bad, could you—"

"List your many failures? Of course," Caleb said. "It is what I am here for. Now, let us begin with the obvious. Your carving and handling of your tools is at best subpar. I would say it is an insult to your tools, but considering you spent all of five dollars on them, it would be too great a compliment to the tools themselves. You do realize that any self-respecting mage spends significant funds on purchasing proper equipment?"

I sighed as I pulled out a notebook, getting ready to listen to Caleb preach about the greatness and magnificence of mages once more. Proper mages. Not weird, sorcerer-mage wish hybrids like me. Because, as bad as this might be for my self-respect, the man knew his work. And—I had to admit—was probably right.

And I did kind of want a self-immolating, inscription wand.

***

"And that should be sufficient to help you improve your design by at least threefold," Caleb said, finishing his lecture.

I stared at the multiples pages of notes I had taken, of which I understood maybe a fifth of and might only be able to afford a quarter of, and could not help but nod. The sad fact was I knew Caleb had even more knowledge to impart on this matter, but considering the sheer difference in knowledge between the two of us, he'd dumbed it down.

"Once again, you have managed to distract me from the planned lesson."

"Sorry, not sorry?" I said with a smirk and a shrug of my shoulders. "I actually had another request."

"Of course you do. What is it now?"

"Rituals. I'm on a quest with Alexa, and we're dealing with a containment ritual and enchantment. It's been damaged though, so I need to restore it," I said.

"The Brixton Orphanage."

"Yes, how did you know?"

"I am the master mage in charge of this region," Caleb said with a sniff. "Part of my duties do require me to be aware of such matters."

"So do you know what is contained by the orphanage?" I asked, curiosity getting the better of me. After all, Alexa had no idea, and the Templars weren't going to tell me.

"That I do not," Caleb said stiffly. "The Templars are not forthcoming about their activities for obvious reasons. I do know that whatever is contained most likely should stay contained."

"Most likely?"

"The Templars are less forgiving than we are," Caleb said. "And considering when this occurred, well, times have changed."

"Ah…" I considered what Caleb meant. I guess society had changed since the sixties, and what was considered acceptable back then and now has altered, at least in most parts of the world. It would stand to reason that changes in social mores among mundanes would also affect tolerance levels among supernaturals. How much of a crossover, I'd have to research. But—"Is there a way to tell? There's a bit of mana leaking out."

"Hmmm… You mean the mana that is produced is tainted by the creature's or item's aura," Caleb said, correcting me. "But yes, there are ways. With your skill set… Marissa's Multibox of Telling would be best."

"The what?"

"Marissa's Multibox of Telling." Caleb walked toward his library of books. He flipped through a few before finding the one he wanted. With an absent toss of his hand, the book landed on a bookstand where Caleb then gestured at, directing a pen that had been seated on the bookstand to begin copying the spell. "Now, we were going to discuss rituals. Let us begin with an overview of your current knowledge."

I stared enviously at the scribing tool. I wanted one!

Caleb clapped his hands together. "Mr. Tsien!"

"Sorry. Overview of rituals. Right. They're just elongated spells, aren't they? Drawn onto chalk circles and boosted with various elemental items?"

"That—" Caleb drew a deep breath and glared at the wide-eyed, innocent face I returned to him. "It seems we have a lot of work to do."

***

Baiting Caleb about what he thought of my knowledge about rituals actually had a point beyond mildly amusing me. In truth, while I had some transmitted knowledge, it was mostly ancillary to the spell knowledge provided by Lily. As such, my foundational knowledge left a lot to be desired. Once again, I had to admit the way Lily had "dumped" information into my brain left me with surprisingly large and weird holes. Especially when the jinn herself was a more natural caster. Her understanding of magic had surprising gaps which at times resulted in issues on my end.

My Ward spell, for example, could not actually be directly translated to a barrier, since much of the knowledge provided to me came from a subset of Enochian magic that never bothered with rituals. So while I could—and did—figure out how to enchant with it, translating the knowledge into a ritual was outside my current skillset. And yes, the differences between a ward, a ritual, and an enchantment were small at times, but when I was altering the fundamental forces of nature, that minor gap could be lethal.

Caleb understood my issues after so many months training me. It was why he was, at times, over-thorough in his explanations. And while I saw no move in my ritual knowledge talents, I knew I had a much firmer grasp of the basics. If we kept these lessons up, in a short while, I would have a much better idea of what to do about the broken enchantments and ritual. Of course…

"Why aren't you fixing the enchantments?" I asked Caleb as we wrapped up the lesson plan.

"What do you mean?"

"Well, isn't it your job?"

"Again, you misunderstand my role. I am to watch for and deal with significant threats. While whatever is trapped by the Templars in the orphanage is of note, it is not, as you have pointed out, inherently violent. As such, it is outside of my area of responsibility. What would my life be like if I went around dealing with every minor issue third-rate sorcerers created? No. Whatever is down there is something the Templars can handle themselves."

"And if it's an item?"

"Then taking it away if it is dangerous would be simpler after its release."

"And you don't want to be bothered."

"And I don't want to be bothered." Caleb affably agreed. "You will find as you progress that many of the concerns you exhibit now are less important. They are, in fact, trivial to your progress as a mage."

"For you maybe," I said under my breath, staring at the numerous books that made up the portion of the library Caleb had brought with him. I knew he easily had hundreds more in his actual house. For "real" mages, study and experimentation were more important than going out and "leveling." Whether it was a curse or blessing, I needed to do both. Only through constant and practical use of my spells did the knowledge imparted to me become better integrated.

And truth be told, I might be a bit of a geek, but even I can get tired of reading.

***

Since Caleb had been of little use in understanding what was actually trapped beneath, I figured I would spend some time researching the building. I was curious if the enchantments had been built from the start or something that had appeared recently. It certainly seemed strange that if they were going to add an enchantment to a building, they didn't do what everyone else did: add it in the foundations, out of sight. It made things so much simpler, and stronger in most cases.

With that in mind, I made a visit to the archival room of our public library. It was only when I arrived I found out that not only did they not keep building plans, access to building plans at city hall also required me to get the permission of the owners. Oh, and there was no guarantee they'd have plans for something as old as the orphanage.

"So what can I find out here?" I asked, slightly exasperated.

Thankfully, the librarian—a thin, weedy-looking guy who looked like he needed less time in the sun—didn't take offense with my question and directed me to the microfilm section. There, he then pointed me at the various resources available, patiently explaining that no, there wasn't a web search that would give me all the information contained. And then, the bastard left me.

Four hours later, I recalled why I hated libraries. I gently dropped my head onto the giant tome that blandly described the history of social housing and welfare for children in the city. It was intensely boring, but it did at least mention the orphanage… if not in the context I required.

"May I be of assistance?" a soft voice asked me, and I twitched, tilting my head sideways. Next to me was a bespectacled, bird-headed creature with coffee-colored skin. I stared at the creature for a second, my brain trying to locate the particular type. Its feathered head bobbed slightly as the creature continued to speak. "I am Adom." Lowering his voice even further, Adom said, "I am from my lord Thoth's lineage."

"Oh…" My brain scrambled for a second, thankful for long, long D&D sessions and a rather weird obsession with all things mythological. Thoth was the Egyptian god of knowledge. Details came back from an abandoned campaign, filling in further details. Egyptian gods were generally decent, and since he was just someone from that lineage, I should treat him like any other supe. "Depends. You good at research?"

"I have some small skill," Adom said, inclining his head.

"Perfect," I said with a grin. "I need to know everything you can find about the Brixton Orphanage. In five days."

"Lord mage, I fear you misunderstand. Good research takes time," Adom said, shaking his head disapprovingly.

"I know, but I've got a time-limited quest here, so chop-chop," I said. "Not that I mean you should. Ummm… how much would I owe you?"

Adom cocked his head to the side now, regarding me for a time. "Five days of dedicated research. Rush order. Two thousand dollars."

"Two thousand!" I yelped and got glares from the few people around. I simmered down, shooting a sheepish glance back at the library attendees I had disturbed. "That's daylight robbery. One."

"Deal. Should I meet you here or at your offices?" Adom said immediately.

"Wait a second. I feel like I've been cheated here!" I grumbled. Damn it. Luckily, this was real life, or I'd probably receive negative experience for negotiating. "And here is fine. Probably for the best."

"Pleasure doing business with you," Adom said, offering his hand. I shook it while standing and walked out of the library. A thousand dollars. Gah! At least, if we completed Alexa's quest, we should still see a profit. Still. A thousand dollars.

Cursing myself, I made my way home.

Chapter 11

"Why are we doing this stakeout again?" I grumbled as we sat in the car, in a new spot overlooking the building. This was the second lookout spot we had used in the last few hours, Alexa having decided that moving more often was a better idea than having the police called on us again. Not that I disagreed, but…

"Intelligence before an attack is important. Do we have a Link?" Alexa said and prodded me. I stared at the small circular makeup mirror we had purchased for this very purpose, figuring it was easier than constantly adjusting the rearview mirror.

"Yes. The usual," I said and shifted the mirror for Alexa to look. I swear, these guys desperately needed to find something better to do than stare at the idiot box all day. Who cared what horrible food was being eaten, which long-lost cousin with amnesia was being released from jail, or how to bake a double-chocolate-fudge cake. Actually, maybe the last one.

"Let's just keep watching," Alexa said in reply after she looked.

"Fine. But what are we waiting for?" I said with a grimace. Still, I sat back and focused on feeding mana to the image while doing my utmost to draw in as much mana from the surroundings as possible.

"Either another shipment or payment. They were paid recently, so it's not likely to be the second. But if they receive a second shipment, we can hit them and destroy it. Maybe even take their money at the same time."

"You don't mean to launch the attack when the courier is there, right? Because we're a bit far away to do that…"

"No. We can take the three, but I don't know how many would be with their courier. Or when it'd arrive. Better for us to just destroy their product," Alexa said.

"Actually, I think taking their money would be better. See, the product is probably quite cheap to make, but the money they earn is, well, money."

"Why'd you think it's cheap to make?"

"Isn't that how drugs work? The product is cheap but gets marked up because it's illegal?" I asked with a shrug. "Or gets marked up because of the cost of lost product due to law enforcement, which in this case would be us."

Alexa frowned at my words but, after a moment's consideration, slowly nodded.

"Great. Then let's go home, and we'll plan the hit."

"Can we not talk about it like that?" Alexa asked. "We're not assassins."

"Fine," I said, maybe a bit pitifully. I guessed she wouldn't accept wearing black masks too?

***

"Masks are a good idea," Alexa said with a nod. "I'll put up my hair and wear a wig too."

"Wait. You're good with a mask?"

"Of course." Alexa nodded firmly. "We don't want to be caught. And you should put a glamour on us too. Just in case."

"Sure," I said, readjusting my thinking. I then stared at the sketched-out map of the house before us on my grid paper. Who said buying all this erasable grid paper for my RPG games had been a waste? Har! Though, when I had pulled it out, I'd realized how long it had been since I had a good game. Ever since my last group broke up due to interpersonal conflicts—seriously, how many times did we have to repeat "do not date in your game group" before people got it—I hadn't had a good game. Then again, I was living an urban fantasy campaign. But… well, there was still something missing.

On the grid map, we'd sketched the inner layout of the building as best as we could gather from my repeated uses of Scry. Added on to it, we had another section for the second floor. Theoretically we should have had one more for the basement, but considering we'd never seen the basement itself, it was currently empty.

On top of all this, we had a printout of the satellite image for the neighborhood and a map of the roads around the location itself including one-way streets, exits to the nearest highway, and other viable and contingency roads. I'd also taken the time to mark where the nearest police station was, though as we'd found out, the police did have a few roaming patrols.

"I'm not sure if I'm impressed or disturbed by how competent you are planning a robbery," Alexa said, watching as I jotted further information onto the map.

"Blame Shadowrun," I said.

Lily snorted at that, while Alexa looked at me blankly.

"This is so a Shadowrun job. You're even going to go in the front door, guns blazing!" Lily giggled.

"There are no guns. Wait, are there guns, Henry?" Alexa asked, staring at me.

"No guns. It's just a saying." I cocked my head sideways at Lily. "Though I'm surprised someone knows it."

"I like reading fanfic," Lily said. "And other people's recounting of their games."

"Ah…" I paused, considering the jinn. "You know, you could just sign up to play a game."

"I could?" Lily paused, her gaze turning unconsciously to the ring on my finger. After a moment, she smiled and nodded. "I could!"

"Did… did you just not realize it?"

"You try living a few millennia trapped in a ring," Lily said with her arms crossed. "I forget I can, you know, do things."

"Ahem." Alexa cleared her throat and pointed at the map. "So what are we looking at?"

"Well, if things go bad, we've got about ten minutes before the cops arrive—give or take—from the station. Probably five if there's a roaming patrol car," I said, tapping the map. "The neighborhood is mostly made up of double income earners, so I think going in during the day at around ten would be best. At night, there's a lot more people, so we're more likely to get spotted. Better to do it when everyone's out."

"Sounds fair," Alexa said.

"Right. We go in during the day. If we wait till they're all upstairs, we can walk right up to their front door. If I spend the rest of tonight, I'm pretty sure I can make the equivalent of a lockpick," I said. "Which will get us in the front door. Then we just have to—" That's when I stopped, realization hitting me.

"We'll have to deal with them."

"Right. Yeah…" My brain stuttered to a stop again, a pause that made Alexa frown at me.

"What's wrong, Henry?"

"I'm not sure about our plan. If they resist, we're going to have fight them. They've got guns and…" I paused, drawing a shuddering breath. "And I don't know if I can put them down without killing them. If I'm willing to kill them. If I can. What if I freeze? What if you get shot while I freeze? What happens if my shields can't hold up against the bullets? What if the bullets bounce and hit them? What—"

"Henry." A hand falls on my arm, squeezing it so tight, my breath hitches and my rambling stops. "You haven't killed before, have you?"

"Yes, I have," I said in protest.

"I don't mean rats. Or demons. Or obvious monsters," Alexa said. "I mean humans. Or those close to them."

"I…" I shook my head. "Why is it so different?"

"Because it is." Alexa shrugged. "We all have our own mental hiccups. It's not a bad thing. It doesn't make you weak. But I need you to think about this, very carefully. Before we make any more plans, I need you to know where your lines are."

"And if I can't kill them?" I whispered softly.

"Then we'll know. And plan around that," Alexa said.

I nodded dumbly and took my arm back from her. I realized with a shock that my hands were shaking, adrenaline setting my nerves tingling and my heartbeat rocketing without any real escape. I stumbled to the couch and sat down heavily, breathing slowly as my mind spiraled.

Could I kill? Should I kill? They were gangsters. Drug dealers. Bad people. But I wasn't the Punisher. I was no soldier who got up in the morning and chanted songs about shooting my enemies in the head. I was a gamer given a gift, and

I'd mostly used it to do good. Sure, I'd been in a few fights, but killing a demon or Devil Rats wasn't morally reprehensible. They were pests. And demons. I'd have to be really messed up to have a moral problem with killing demons.

I paused, realizing I was shying away from the topic at hand once again. Killing humans. The drug dealers. Was it right? If they tried to kill me, sure. I could do that. Eye for an eye. No problem. In the heat of battle, it made sense. But here, I was planning to break into their house and fight them. It was so cold. So, wrong.

Was that why the law had differences between premeditated murder and murders of passion? Because planning and acting on a plan was so much worse? That you had to steel yourself to do it? But weren't these drug dealers doing the same? With their drugs.

Where do we—do I—draw the line? I was no saint. I wasn't going to say I would never kill. That only worked in comics. Hell, considering how much damage Batman did on a regular basis to the average mugger, in the real world, he'd eventually accidentally kill someone from a medical complication, an unknown heart condition, a seizure, a blood clot entering the brain. Humans were fragile.

But it didn't mean I was about to go around killing others. Or that I should. Somewhere, somehow, there should be a line. At least for me.

I sat on the couch, staring onto the busy city street while pondering exactly where I drew the line in my new life. Where do I, Henry Tsien, mage, decide it was okay to take a life.

***

Hours later, I looked up as dinner was set in front of me. This time around, it was Alexa's turn to cook, which resulted in tasty but simple tomato, ground-meat pasta. As the still-steaming dish sat in front of me, taunting my empty belly, Alexa took a seat before me and spoke.

"Are you okay?"

"Yes. I think. I guess, I just never really thought about what it meant," I said softly. "Getting jumped and attacked by orcs or werejackals was one thing. I could justify doing whatever I needed to do to guard myself. And if it was scary, well, what hasn't been? But breaking and entering… killing people. The morality of it is a lot greyer when it's real life."

Alexa cocked her head to the side for a time before she nodded slowly. "It's one thing I admire and pity about you, Henry. Your innocence, your optimism and belief in people. While we were taught that everyone is loved by God, we were also trained to kill, to see supernaturals as less than human. Even other humans, those who dabbled in magic and the supernatural world, were considered tainted, unworthy.

"It was simple, theoretically. I was a faith healer. It wasn't as if I was supposed to fight them directly. While we all received the training, for me, it was less real. Then I was sent to you, and we've interacted with—done quests—for the supernatural. Talked to them. Done wards for their newborns and light shows for their graduation parties. They stopped all being monsters, but…"

"But?"

"But the bad ones are still bad. The Templars are here to stop those who are bad, who are wrong. Whether it's dealing drugs or killing people, if they're human or supernatural. If they're doing evil, my job—our job is to stop them," Alexa said.

"But I'm not a Templar."

"No. You're not."

I rubbed my face again, picking up my fork to twirl the pasta around as a distraction. After a time, I shook my head and dropped it. "I don't think I can choose to do that, Alexa. I know what they're doing is wrong. I know it. But killing them when they're not trying to kill me, I can't do it."

"Then let's plan to capture them," Alexa said simply. "If we have time, I can have the Knights take them in."

"Kill them," I stated with some horror in my voice.

"Not necessarily," Alexa said. "I'm sure they'd have information we could use."

"Like?"

"Their supplier. Who they work for. Their goals," Alexa rattled off.

"Oh…" I could push her, ask what happened when all that information was given, when they had learned everything they wanted. But really, I knew that answer too. And somehow, I had to admit, I was willing to let it happen. Perhaps it was hypocritical of me, to condemn men to death but not want the blood itself on my hand. But if so, it was a level of hypocrisy I could live with. And sleep with.

"Capture." I prodded the pasta again and then firmly nodded. "If we're going to do that, I better get planning."

Alexa smiled at my words, nodding slightly and sitting backward. Off to the side, I caught Lily frowning slightly as she tapped away at her computer, but she said nothing, at least not yet.

It was only later that night when Alexa had retired for the evening and I had come back downstairs, my mind still whirling with minor alterations to the plan when the jinn spoke.

"Are you really okay with this?" Lily asked as I pushed the little robed mage and paladin miniatures around the board.

"What? The plan. Of course, I made it."

"Doing the Templars' bidding," Lily said, tapping her keyboard to pause her game and turn directly toward me. "It's not really your quest. You don't have any personal penalties for failing."

"Except I might lose Alexa."

"Except that," Lily said, conceding my point. "But while she might be friendly now, do remember that her job is to keep an eye on you and to keep you alive till you hit level one hundred, and the ring can come off."

"At which point everyone and their boss is going to come after me," I said flatly. "I remember. And that's why… That's why I need to do this."

Lily hummed slightly, prompting me to go on, and I sighed.

"I'm not a killer, Lily. I mean, sure. I've killed imps. And the demon. And Devil Rats and evil ravens. And those weird llama creatures," I said, ticking off the violence I'd conducted in my time. "But I'm not a killer. Not like her Templars. Or the orcs. Or the werejackals. I wasn't brought up to kill."

"So, you're going to make it clear to them you won't kill?" Lily asked, slightly incredulously. "How's that going to help you survive?"

"Because if I'm going to survive, I'm going to need to push myself, and killing them is easy. Simple. But my life isn't going to be simple, and this isn't going to be easy," I said slowly, reaching inside to explain a thought process I had barely grasped. "If—when I hit level one hundred, when the ring comes off, I'm going to have to fight them all. If I can learn to handle myself now with gloves on, maybe I'll be able to handle them all when the gloves come off."

Lily smiled sadly at me at my words but said nothing further. I knew—as she probably did—I had a naïve hope. But surviving when I hit level one hundred was a naïve hope. I already had two major groups gunning for me, and obviously more to come. But hope, naïve and hopeless as it may be, was all I had.

***

The drive to the drug house the next morning was quiet, tense. I found myself patting my coat repeatedly, a nervous motion as I tried to assess what the hell I was missing. It was stupid, since I had literally created a long list of everything I would need and ticked them off earlier this morning. Then I wiped down and burned anything that might be incriminating.

"Stop it. Nothing has changed since the last minute," Alexa said grumpily.

"Sorry." I put my hands down. "Right. In five minutes, I'll throw the glamour and illusion on us to hide who we are. I'll do the same with the car too, so they can't track the vehicle. Then—"

"Henry. We've gone over this a hundred times. We'll be fine," Alexa said, making me slowly fall silent. I knew she was right, but I felt the urge to snap at her, a feeling I pushed down with a surge of willpower that I was quite proud of. Truth be told, I knew I was being irrational.

"Right. Right." I fell silent, and a few moments later, I started going over the list of items I had brought with me.

"Five minutes," Alexa said, interrupting me as I mentally went over what I had brought for the umpteenth time.

I drew a deep breath and exhaled while channeling an illusion over the car. It wasn't a complex illusion, just minor changes like shifting the color of the car itself and the license plate along with removing any dents, scratches, and other, potentially identifiable material. After I sent a surge of mana into the car and completed the spell, I turned toward Alexa and nodded. Together, we tapped the small wooden enchantment I had created last night to store a simple glamour and illusion. In both cases, I went for boring and generic, making Alexa look older, brunette, and less striking while I made myself Caucasian, brunette, and older too.

As the car drew closer to the house, I took a moment to connect to the mirrors one last time to check that the three within were at their usual spots. Thankfully, they were, allowing us to carry on our nefarious task immediately.

Step one: Park the car and approach the house directly and cleanly, without acting suspicious and shifty. I made sure to grab my backpack and slung it over one shoulder, while Alexa carried her broken-down spear in a simple sports bag. When we approached the house, I moved to block Alexa from the view of any neighbors while casting a simple illusion spell over the house's video surveillance camera. A moment later, Alexa had the door open with her lockpicks.

I actually felt bad about my boast. Once I actually thought about the requirements to pick a lock magically, I realized I had neither the spells, the knowledge, nor the time to perfect an enchantable tool. Online videos showing how to move pins and tumblers were one thing, but having a force spell that could not only adjust the degree, angle, and speed of force applied to tiny little metal pieces was beyond me. Alexa had had a good laugh late last night when I started grumbling about the matter before she informed me about her skillset.

Step two was simple. Once inside, a quick scry verified our targets were still in the same location. While I did that, Alexa put together her spear, getting ready for the violence about to occur. At the same time, I ran through the spell formulas I'd created just for this moment before releasing the Scry spell. If all went well, no one was going to die.

Step three required actual action. I snuck up first, doing my best Sneaky Pete impression. Of course, I wasn't exactly trained to sneak, but I'd been a kid. Recalling the rules we'd used while playing ninja at home, I made sure not to walk in the middle of the staircase while crouching low as we ascended. When I reached the second floor, I poked my head around the corner of the staircase to see the three sprawled in the open living room, still staring at the TV.

Once again, I started a spell formula in my mind. This time I was prepping a Force Bolt, but instead of a single spherical container, I was going for a longer, cylindrical container, one that was slightly flexible. I called it my Force Rope, and in theory, the replication of the spell three times would let me wrap the three humans up without a problem.

The first two spells formed in my mind, then I began the third. Since these were all the same spell, it was difficult but not impossible, unlike triple casting three different spells. Here, at least, I just needed to concentrate on keeping the threads of mana and the spell formulas in mind.

Loud, incessant blaring of the horn from outside broke my concentration, forcing the third spell to come apart. I almost lost the other two as well, the feedback from the broken spell making me clench my teeth and let out a huff. Luckily, the noise I made was hidden by the continual honking.

"Shit. Is it delivery day?" a voice growled from above. Chairs creaked as our targets stood. I shared a wide-eyed, shocked look with Alexa as our plans came apart in moments. For a second, we both stood there in shock, footsteps coming closer before Alexa acted and rushed upward, jostling me aside gently and forcing me to struggle to hold the spells again.

"Wha—Urkk," the voice screamed, the squark and gurgled ending an auditory clue of what happened. I had no more time, no gap to consider our bad luck. It was time to act.

I strode upward, looking for and finding my targets. One was reaching for a shotgun down by his chair, the second was attempting to ward off Alexa's spear with his free hand while he vainly grasped for a handgun in his pants, and the other lay on the ground, his throat slashed. I dismissed the second, focusing on the first as I adjusted the range coordinates of my spell.

"Force Chain!" I called, releasing the spell with an auditory component. I held back the second spell, already weaving the spell formula to adjust the range to something a lot closer. Not that it was necessary. Alexa had cut the man's hand open, then swept in and kicked his bladder region, right on top of the gun which the gangster was vainly attempting to draw.

My Force Chain flew outward, wrapping the first gangster's arms and body around the lounge chair he had been sitting upon. He screamed as the chain yanked tight, plush and wooden components of the chair creaking as my hastily reconstructed spell formulas restricted his motion a little too much. He shouted in pain and surprise, a noise that set my teeth on edge. A Force Ball, located right in his mouth, worked as a useful if somewhat transparent ball gag.

As I turned toward Alexa and her opponents, I noticed she had thrust the spear into the second man's neck, this time nicking open veins and arteries. Gripping his throat, the man gurgled as his blood flowed out, unable to make much more noise than Alexa's first victim.

"Secure him!" Alexa snapped at me as I stared at the growing pool of blood. I twisted around and saw my own target had tipped his chair to the side and fallen to the ground, still bound tight as he futilely struggled toward his shotgun.

I rushed toward him and kicked the weapon away before I secured the man's feet together using a series of zip ties. I frowned, realizing I could either release him and then attempt to forcefully yank his arms together to secure them again or I could leave him as he was, tied to the chair by magic. I knew it wasn't the most secure method either. The chair was too large and plush, too pliant for there to be a truly secure binding. With a grimace, I made note to look into a sleeping spell before I recast a second Force Rope, sliding this one over both his shoulders and between his legs like a weird five-point harness.

"Come on!" Alexa snarled from downstairs. I refocused, listening to the garage doors sliding open downstairs, and hurried to the first floor, my feet making squelching sounds in the blood when I rushed past. My stomach roiled for a second, reminding me there were now two men who were dying, who I was leaving behind, but—

"I'll close the garage doors first. Have a Force Ball ready. I'll take the first person to come out. You deal with the second!" Alexa ordered me as she crouched beside the door to the garage, the garage remote still held tight in her hand. Almost immediately after it stopped grinding, she tapped the button, forcing it closed again. "Get ready."

I nodded, focusing within as I readied a Force Spear, rounding the tip to ensure it didn't kill the individual immediately. A part of me wondered if I should cast Scry to check out how many people we would be expecting, but we had only seconds left and no mirror in easy access. I discarded the idea and forced myself to draw a deep breath once again, the thrum of a readied spell riding in my mind.

"Mario!" a surprisingly high-pitched voice called from inside the garage. A moment later, the doorknob shook and the door swung open, revealing a surprised-looking human. Except, on second look, I noticed the creature had no philtrum beneath its nose, and its skin glowed slightly with a faint golden radiance. Before I could take in the creature, Alexa swung her spear at it. Only, a reflexive block with the sports bag he held in hand saved the creature from being skewered.

"Who are you!" The creature snarled, falling backward as he blocked Alexa's attacks with his bag. That golden radiance seemed to concentrate around its forehead, growing in intensity. With a snarl, I raised my hand and released the Force

Spear before whatever spell, curse, or other ability was engaged.

Diwata (Level 38)
HP 138/138

The diwata jerked its head sideways in a vain attempt to dodge the Force Bolt at the last second. The Force Bolt clipped the side of its head, making the monster stumble backward, at which point Alexa's thrust tore into its shoulder. The initiate pushed forward as she attempted to keep the creature off balance, the pair entering the garage where she was shoulder-checked by a larger humanoid.

Immediately, I scrambled to the door to see Alexa pinned against wooden shelves of the garage and being punched repeatedly by a linebacker-sized orc, his polyurethane sports jacket sporting the logo of a familiar football team. But I had little time to watch, for the diwata had turned its attention toward me, the glow returning to its forehead.

"Shield!" I snarled, my hand rising and fingers splaying, and my shield took the blast of magical energy straight on. I staggered as the creature pressed its advantage and continually pummeled my spell's screen with its own magic. Over the brilliance of the attack, I squinted in a desperate attempt to see what was happening within.

Unable to see past my now-opaque shield, I raised my other hand and began to cast a Force Bolt, using the simpler version of my spell to allow me to multiply the number of Force Bolts in it. I then launched them blindly through the garage door, hoping Alexa was still in her corner. For a moment, the pressure on my Shield relented but then returned twofold. Cracks appeared all across it as my concentration wavered, my mana draining rapidly.

"Damn it!" I growled and held both hands up, flooding mana through them to reinforce the Shield. It held again, but a short, strangled scream from within let me know my friend needed my help. Fast. I swallowed, warm iron-tasting liquid sliding down my throat from a bit tongue as I forced myself to focus.

I couldn't see within to cast a spell. I couldn't even divert mana to do so. There was no guarantee my Shield and mana would last longer than the diwata within, but I had to act. I had to push in.

Push.

Oh. I kicked myself mentally and focused on the spell formula, searching quickly within my mind for the appropriate section. It was strange, how the channeled spell seemed to have a physical presence within my mind, like a glowing text twisted and wrapped together that mana flowed through. A channel I only needed to locate and adjust. In this case, the positioning portion of the spell.

I tied off other parts of the spell, fixing the sections dictating the shield's size and orientation. Using my body as the initial point for the coordinates, I pushed my now-tied-off shield forward, changing its location quickly. I basically turned the entire Force Shield into a moving projectile, one I constantly fed with mana. A loud intake of breath and a sudden pressure informed me my actions had been noticed, but too late. The impact of the Shield on the diwata's body rocked me mentally, but thankfully, the creature's attack cut off soon after impact.

I didn't relent even then. Drawing on my mana further, I shoved the Shield forward, pinning the creature onto the hood of the parked vehicle in the garage. I felt the sudden loss of pressure on the top, even as my Shield refused to move farther as its legs were crushed and trapped. The diwata let out a strangled scream even as the spell slowly dissipated. I had no time for the monster as I rushed into the garage from the house and spotted Alexa.

The initiate was doing less than well, her shoulder pinned to the wall via her own spear. The pair struggled over the shaft of it, the larger orc looming over the initiate as it dragged the spear relentlessly from Alexa's grasp.

"DIE!" I shouted as I flung my hand up and called forth an Iceball. I mentally adjusted the spell, making the container slightly sharper and more pointed, and I launched the attack into the back of the orc's head. Unfortunately, my scream alerted the creature, and he ducked even lower, letting the Iceball impact right above Alexa's wide eyes.

"Not me!" Alexa screamed but took the momentary lapse in concentration by the orc to launch a knee between its legs. The orc folded even farther, his grip loosening on the spear which allowed Alexa a chance to rip it from her shoulder properly. Even as she readied to stab the spear downward, I launched a Force Spear into the orc's lower back, the attack digging through his body and entering the bent-over creature's chest cavity from behind.

As the orc tumbled away from Alexa after a forceful push, she looked up with gratitude at me and then threw the spear. I twisted to the side, only to see the diwata stagger backward, its legs healed again with the spear in its chest.

"What?" My jaw dropped open, knowing I had seen and felt its legs being crushed by my Shield. With a shake of my head, I stumbled toward it and ripped the spear out of its body, then slammed it into the monster's chest again, piercing its heart. The creature spasmed once more and stopped, and I found myself exhaling with relief. Unlike the diwata, the orc lay on the ground, bleeding out while Alexa held a glowing white hand up to her shoulder.

"You okay?"

"No!" Alexa snapped. I nodded dumbly, staggering toward her and raising my hand to cast

Heal. "Don't bother. The chainmail vest kept most of it from going in. My healing will have it fixed in a few minutes. You keep your mana."

I nodded dumbly again, grateful I didn't have to tap my already low reserves of mana.

"I'll…" I paused, considering what to do and then pointed up the stairs. Alexa's jerky nod made me smile grimly as I strode up the stairs, my heart still pounding and my hands trembling. Only when I got upstairs and ascertained the last remaining, living member of the criminal group was still tied up did I slump to the ground, my hands trembling.

Oh gods. She had nearly died. I had nearly died.

Chapter 12

It took me a few minutes to get over the sudden violence, the death we had brought upon these living, breathing, sentient humans and supernaturals. Once the initial shock wore off and the adrenaline had reduced, I stood and looked out the window. Thankfully, there seemed to be no movement from the other houses, no twitching curtains or busybody neighbors. It seemed that while our little fight had seemed intensely noisy to me, it had not drawn undue attention. Either that or someone was on the phone already making calls to the police.

In the time I took to settle, I noticed I was not the only one who had calmed—our prisoner was lying on the ground quietly, staring at me. Occasionally, I glimpsed him straining against the Force Chain before relaxing having gotten nowhere. With a grim smile, I stepped past him to collect the weapons. I unloaded the shotgun and the pistols gingerly, pocketed the bullets, and tossed the weapons into a shopping bag I had located.

"Henry?" Alexa called up to me as she ascended the stairs. "Oh, good idea. Did you find the money yet?"

"Not yet," I said. "I was, uhh, not yet." I flushed slightly, deciding not to inform her about my momentary loss of control. I'm sure she would understand. She had the previous few times I'd had a "blind moment." But still, my pride had taken sufficient battering today. "I'll take a look."

"Sure. But mind dismissing his ball gag first?"

I gestured toward the man, dismissing the simple woven ball of power that had been affixed to his mouth. The man spat and wiped his face against his shoulder once again, clearing the drool from his mouth as Alexa yanked the chair up. Only a slight hiss from the initiate gave any indication she had been injured earlier. Well, other than the bloody shirt she wore.

"Now, let's talk."

"You think I'm scared of you, girlie?"

The loud crack of the spear haft when it struck the man followed me into the bedroom as I walked in. I shut the door, blocking out the sounds from the questioning, and I began to inspect the room. Well, ransack it was perhaps a better word. Of course, I made sure to put on a new pair of gloves first, the original pair looking somewhat worse for wear after our earlier battles.

Unfortunately, the room itself held little of interest unless you had an ardent desire for smelly male socks and underwear. Which, I guess, might be a kink, but I would also guess it was an unprofitable one to cater to. For a second, I almost pulled out my phone to check, but using the greater level of self-control that studying magic had provided me, I focused on my search.

When I was done with the room, I moved to the next, and it was there I found the jackpot. A single, large safe sat closed in the closet, awaiting a master safe cracker. Of course, that was not me.

"Alexa, got a safe here," I called to the initiate when I walked out.

Alexa smiled at that, turning back toward the human with a predatory look. Bleeding from a split lip and broken nose, the man glared at Alexa and kept his mouth shut.

"Check their wallets. Or around the safe. I'm willing to bet these dumbasses have it written somewhere," Alexa said to me, her eyes focused on the man. When he glanced downward, toward the stairways, Alexa snorted. "Or maybe the fridge?"

The man's eyes widened slightly, enough that even I caught it.

"They really that dumb?" I muttered as I trooped down the stairs, taking care not to walk through the growing puddle of blood. I knew we had to do something about all that, but right now, it escaped me. I didn't exactly have any useful spells for such a situation.

In minutes, I was back upstairs holding the Post-it Note with the combination that had been handily stuck to the fridge with a Walk Away Fatty fridge magnet. I wondered which one of the three had purchased it as I spun the safe. It took me three tries, once for going the wrong way and the second for missing a number, before I had the safe open. I guess if they had been smart enough to do things like understand basic operational security, they wouldn't be crooks.

Or dead.

As I reached within to pull the stacked cash into the black sports bag I had located, my hand started trembling again. I forcibly drew a breath and exhaled, taking control of my stray thoughts and putting them aside for now. Better to avoid it.

"You think you're going to get away with this? You don't know who you're dealing with! They'll kill you. They're not human!" the man shouted, struggling in his chair. "You're crazy."

"Why don't you tell me all about it then? Who these people are," Alexa said, taunting the man.

"You don't get it. They'll kill me. And you. Or worse!"

"What's worse than death? Well, beyond torture," Alexa said, and a slightly high yelp followed her words soon after. "Hush… you don't want me to have to gag you again, do you?"

"They'll tear your soul out. They use magic!"

"You're really not very smart, are you?" I said when I walked back in the room, weighed down by the hefty bag of ill-gotten funds. "What do you think I was casting?"

The man paused, looked down at how he was held tight and then started thrashing around in his chair, screaming about the devil. Alexa grabbed a sock and shoved it into his mouth, stuffing it in before she glared at me.

"You had to remind him."

"How was I to know he was that stupid!" I said.

"You just opened their safe using a Post-it Note from their kitchen."

"Touché." With a glance at the now-still, cooling corpses, I said slowly, "We might have a problem."

"Not a problem. I've already called my supervisors. They're on their way."

"Isn't this, you know, part of your test?"

"No," Alexa said with a frown. "Why would I need to be tested on how to dispose of their corpses? Don't you know certain supernatural bodies need to be carefully handled? A mutant zombie thrown into the nearby river could cause significant problems. Better to let the experts handle it. Even Templar Ignis would not fail me over the proper use of our resources and training."

"Oh," I said, blinking. Well, duh. "So, about him?"

"They'll handle it," Alexa said. With the man secured, she walked to the couch and sat, drawing a bag toward her. From it, she extracted a pair of wallets. She opened them and perused the cards within, frowning slightly as she tossed out the driver's licenses from both.

"Problem?"

"Yes," Alexa said.

When she refused to elaborate, I walked over to take a look at the licenses. Oh. That made sense. They were from Ashland, down south. While not technically the capital of crime in our little state, it only was a technicality because no politician was going to give out those kinds of awards. It'd be like delivering a Darwin award to the mother of a child. Cruel and unnecessary.

"There a big supernatural presence down there?" I asked Alexa who let out a choked laugh, one that stopped only when she realized I was not joking.

"Is the ocean wet?" Alexa asked rhetorically. "But it's more than that. The supernaturals who hold sway there, they're the worsti kind. Ancient vampires, gangs of shifters, blood sorcerers, and demonic cults all thrive in that city. Doesn't matter how many times the mages or the Templars or anyone else cleanses the place, they just come back."

"You don't stay?" I asked.

"Limited resources," Alexa said. "We'd need to devote a significant number of people to just keep the lid on it. Never mind the fact that a small presence would just be killed in weeks. Anyway, there's always another demon cult, another ancient monster waking from its sleep, or an artifact that needs containing somewhere else."

I grimaced at the last, knowing it was a rather pointed example. Not that we had caused much trouble, Lily and me, but the potential for trouble was what made them fear us, forced them to devote their forces. Though, sometimes, I wondered if they really needed as many watchers as I felt there were.

"The drugs?"

"Are downstairs, in the van. I checked and then left them there," Alexa said.

I nodded and frowned at the bodies and the slowly growing pool of blood. With no trouble coming, I raised my hand and cast Freeze at the corpses, lowering their body temperature and freezing the blood in the bodies and on the ground. Might as well make things easier.

Alexa offered me a slight nod at that, intent on studying the content of the wallets. I watched her for a second more before deciding to head downstairs. Better to hang out in the living room, even if the curtains were drawn, than this room with its corpses. Better to put it out of mind, what I had done.

Sometimes, I wondered if I had made the right wish. If, having given up my mundane life, I also had to give up some of the same morality, some of the beliefs I had previously held. I'd become a killer, someone who took lives without thought. And even if they weren't good people, I sometimes wondered what it meant about me that I was still willing to do so.

***

In a few hours, Alexa's people arrived. It did not take long for them to kick us out, happy to agree we had done our part in tracking down and dealing with the latest shipment. This was but a finger in the dike, but it was sufficient, at least, to be considered completed for her quest, especially since we left them a living, breathing source. Surprisingly, they did not ask about the bag of money I carried out. Then again, it was possible Alexa had informed them of its eventual destination—the coffers of the Brixton Orphanage. Killing two birds with one stone.

Later that evening when Alexa left to donate the ill-gotten funds and check on the repairs, my thoughts once again spiraled. It was a light kick on my shin that drew my attention back from contemplating the depths of my moral depravity.

"Stop it," Lily said.

"Stop what?"

"Brooding. So you killed some bad people. It's not as if you're flaying babies to make a book cover," the jinn said as she sat on the living room table across from me, propping her head on her hands.

"That's an interesting example."

"I've had a lot of owners," Lily said unapologetically. "And you, my dear, are nowhere near the worst. Not even the most naïve. Those rarely survive the week."

I grunted, rubbing my leg. "But killing—"

"Is bad. I know," Lily said with a sniff. "That's what your modern society says, but then they still teach your soldiers how to kill, give guns to your policemen, and have the death sentence for crimes."

"So, what? Violence is part of humanity?"

"Violence is part of the world," Lily said. "Even your vegans kill plants to survive. Ask any treant and they'd call that as a bad if not worse crime than humanity's war. Humans have killed each other all their lives, for all sorts of reasons. Your body fights off viruses and bacteria every moment of your life to keep you alive. Killing, removing the threats from society's body, it's not wrong."

"But what right do I have to make that decision?" I said, grimacing.

"Did they try to kill you?"

"After we broke in!"

"After they started dealing in a dangerous, nasty drug."

"Well… yes," I said slowly. "But—"

"Did you check first? Did you see them selling the drugs? Did they go for their guns first?"

"Yes…"

"Then," Lily said, tapping me on the head, "You did your homework. You verified they were bad guys. You even went in with a plan to avoid killing them. That things went wrong is not your fault. They went for their guns. The rest was natural consequence."

"I just…" I opened my mouth to protest and was shushed by fingers on my lips. I glared at the jinn, tempted to bite the fingers which were hastily removed.

"Henry, stop thinking about how you should be feeling. Actually consider. Are you actually upset you killed them or upset because you believe you should be upset?"

"That—"

"Think! Or feel," Lily commanded me, and I grunted, leaning backward and crossing my arms over my chest. Still, I eventually repressed the surge of anger and actually considered her words.

Did I really feel bad? Actually feel bad? Maybe a little. Not for them but for whatever family they might have had. But they'd made their decision. They'd chosen to live their lives by the sword. And so, was it so surprising they'd die by the sword? Or spear in this case. Did I feel bad they'd died?

No.

I was just upset because somehow, somewhere, I thought I should be. I'd done the best I could to stop them from dying, from being killed. It hadn't played out the way I'd wanted, and now it was over. They were dead, but it wasn't something I truly regretted. Once I realized that, I found my chest relaxing slightly, tension I had carried in my neck disappearing. I grimaced, realizing what it meant but dismissed the thought a moment later. Fine. Maybe I was so focused on the type of person I should be that I got myself churned up for not meeting this random belief.

But...

"I'm still worried," I said, touching my heart. "I… They died, and they left people who will grieve for them. And I know it's their choice, but…"

"But?"

"But it's not about them," I said through a breath, my hands no longer trembling. I looked at Lily, my eyes wide, and bent to kiss her head suddenly. "Thank you. But I've got to go."

Lily looked shocked for a second at the kiss as I walked toward the exit, fishing in my pocket for my mobile phone while putting my jacket on.

"Ma? Everything's fine! I just wanted to see if you're free for dinner tonight. No, it's fine. No, I'm not getting married. Ma!"

***

Later that evening—much later—I returned and found Lily seated at her usual place in the living room, tapping away at the keyboard and moving her mouse around, occasionally shifting her gaze to the other laptop. I shut the door silently and tiptoed toward the stairs, not wanting to disturb her. I nearly made it too.

"Did you tell them?"

I paused, hand on the banister. I considered the evening—dinner with my family where my mom had cooked an extra helping of stewed soya pork, steamed bak choy, fried fish, and rice for my sudden appearance; how my parents had spoken of their work, the usual grind and politics of working in the office; and we had, as always, stayed away from the touchy topic of my employment—or lack of it. We had talked and reminisced, gossiped about my siblings and then spent the rest of the evening watching an old kung fu movie, indulging in a shared love for schlocky Shaw brothers' entertainment, but—

"No." My fingers squeezed the railing as I recalled how I lost the nerve time after time. How I failed to let them know what I was doing. The risks I was taking. The potential visit they might receive one day. "I couldn't. They were so happy to see me, and…"

"And?"

"And I didn't want them in this world," I said suddenly, heat growing in my voice. "It's beautiful. And amazing. Wondrous and magical. But they were worried because I was taking the bus home, afraid I'd get mugged on public transit. If I told them, they'd tell my siblings, and I can't—I won't, get them involved. This world, it's not something I want them in."

"It's hidden for a reason," Lily said, agreeing with me. "The world has moved on, with peace and civil order for everyone but the few and the strange."

I couldn't help but feel the corner of my lips twist at her words. I offered the jinn one last nod before I made my way upstairs to my bed, a part of me amused to realize I was part of the few and strange now. But perhaps before bed, I'd write a letter. One that might explain matters a little more. A just in case, for when and if things went bad.

Chapter 13

"Well, that was a decent attempt. At destroying the neighborhood," Caleb said acerbically, pointing to the revised ritual diagram I had created. I stared at the corrections I had made to the test ritual he had asked me to look over as part of my studies this morning. "You've got channels of power flowing in circles without an exit here, here, and here."

I blinked, following his fingers to where they traced the floating mana formulas I had materialized from the ritual circle as I pumped in a trickle of mana. I watched the flow of it, noting where his finger traced the air and the slowly growing density of mana at the locations and winced.

"Remember, always have an escape valve. No ritual is guaranteed to be done right," Caleb said. "Now release it."

I nodded and altered the formula, releasing the trapped mana back into the ether where the dangerous build-up dispersed. Unlike what most people would think, I didn't power rituals from my own mana. I kickstarted and guided it with my mana, but a ritual, unlike a spell, actually banked on drawing external mana sources to fuel it. After all, why go through all the trouble of carving, formulating, and enchanting a ritual circle if you could cast the spell yourself? You'd save yourself dozens of steps.

No, rituals were made to be powered from external power sources. It was why low-powered sorcerers with a ritual circle were dangerous. Why a runaway ritual was so dangerous. Of course, most rituals just collapsed in on themselves as the materials used to make the circle gave out before a world-ending event happened, but still, the resulting backlash from an exploding ritual circle could—as Caleb pointed out—level a city block. Not all those gas explosions out there are actual gas explosions.

"But aren't those escape valves, the gaps in the formula, weaknesses in the ritual itself?" I asked.

"They are, but if your concern is strength, perhaps you should not be attempting such a ritual anyway," Caleb said. "Just like a door is an entrance to a house, you wouldn't build a house without one, now would you? Fit your ritual strength to what you expect to contain, but always build the door."

I grunted, deciding not to argue further with Caleb. Yet, in the corners of my mind where Lily had stuffed my magical knowledge, I could see formulas and spells, rituals that had been created without any such escape valves. Bindings that were meant to last through the test of time.

"If you're done?" Caleb said, and without waiting for me to answer him, he swept his hand across the ritual, dispersing it. Immediately, the ritual circle began to shift to his commands, adjusting as the circle's enchantments and formulas adjusted to what he had in mind. It was a casual showcase of power and mastery that made me envy the mage.

"Begin."

***

Hours later, I stumbled out of the lesson with spell formulas floating in my mind, arranging and rearranging themselves while I tried to piece it all together. My brain hurt but in a good way, as borrowed knowledge slowly assimilated and I grasped what had been given to me. I was still miles away from being an actual apprentice, but...

Class: Mage
Level 23 (37% Experience)
Known Spells: Light Sphere, Force Spear, Force Shield, Force Fingers, Alter Temperature, Gong, Gust, Heal, Healing Ward, Link, Track, Fix, Ward, Glamour, Illusion, Summon, Iceball, Fireball, Prism, Empower, Scry & Observe, Confuse

Magical Skillset
Mana Flow: 4/10
Mana to Energy Conversion: 4/10
Spell Container: 4/10
Spatial Location: 4/10
Spatial Movement: 4/10
Energy Manipulation: 4/10
Biological Manipulation: 3/10
Matter Manipulation: 2/10

Summoning: 1/10
Duration: 5/10
Rituals: 2/10
Multi-Casting: 2/10
Enchanting: 2/10

Interestingly enough, my spells had not widened significantly. Oh, I had a few more. Prism was actually just a variation of the initial Light Sphere ward but one that basically allowed me to play flashlight in multiple colors. The light itself did nothing beyond split in color, so it was more a utility spell like Fix or Track than a combat spell. But, as I've come to realize, utility spells were probably the most damn useful spells ever. It made me realize how few of them actually existed in my old RPG books. Murder hobos, we all were.

Then again, basic enchanting, which was a new added skillset, probably took care of most needs. After all, the need to layer spells on enchanted objects—like my wooden blocks—was what would make magic truly useful for the populace. When magic—or technology—reached the masses, that's when change really happened. It amused me, somewhat, that I only got Empower now, after I'd gained some basic knowledge of enchanting. Then again, perhaps it was because I had worked out how to enchant myself that Empower was available. The spell basically allowed me to temporarily place an enchantment on an object, bypassing the need to carve or otherwise layer spells on it by using the spell structure of Empower itself as the container for the enchanted spell.

Scry & Observe was just an upgrade on the Scry spell itself, a more complex version that would help with some of the problems I had encountered while using the basic spell. Among other things, I could link the spell across multiple physical objects at the same time, giving me much greater diversity. I knew the next step would actually give me a floating, observing eye, one not linked to any physical surface but that would take a bit to get there.

Lastly, and what I was somewhat stoked about was Confuse. It was my latest spell which had opened a whole new area of magic to me: mind magic. Of course, confuse was the simplest spell and basically bombarded the target's mind with numerous, random thoughts. When I'd woken up this morning with the spell in mind, I could not help but chuckle at it. First devised thousands of years ago, the spell had not altered much in the intervening years until the onset of radio and television. The latest iteration was a minor update, one that would allow me to pull from multiple, random electronic signals, turning my target into basically a giant television receiver.

I had actually considered playing around with the spell when I had time, using some of the knowledge I had garnered from Heal to create targeted neurochemical imbalances and neuron overfiring. Only problem was, I wasn't actually clear what the various portions of the spell did or, for that matter, how to alter the spell without say, blowing up someone's head.

On top of that of course was the issue of bypassing an individual's natural aura resistance. A spell like Confusion worked because it came at things in a slightly sideways fashion, but the sheer mana required to make the spell work was staggering. Unlike, say, Force Bolt, I had to directly bypass my target's aura to have the spell affect them. And while Heal did that too, in most cases, the individual either trusted me to do so and thus "opened" their aura or were unconscious. It basically made the cost lower, though, as I knew from experience, not insignificant. Either way, Confuse now gave me a way to deal with individuals without potentially having to hit, punch, or otherwise hurt them.

Whistling, I made my way back toward the house, only to be brought to a halt by an impatiently waiting Alexa.

"Where have you been?" she demanded.

"Class."

"Why weren't you answering your phone?" Alexa asked, pointing at her parked car. I scrambled to get in as she ducked within.

"Uhh…" I reached for my phone and stared at the blank screen. "Crap. Forgot to charge it. What's the problem?"

"There's an issue at the orphanage. The contractors have damaged the ritual bindings even more," Alexa said, and her lips thinned before she continued. "The abbess mentioned the children are really feeling uneasy now."

I nodded at her words, not surprised. Children were, generally, more sensitive than adults. It mostly had to do with their aura strength being significantly lower but also a wider acceptance of the world. That, unfortunately, came with a cost. It was also the reason old, cantankerous bastards tended to be fine living in haunted locations.

"Is it open?"

"Do you think I'd wait if it was?" Alexa asked with a curl of her lip. I blinked and then nodded, accepting the sense in her words.

"Any further clues about what is in there?" I asked while running through our options. Thankfully, I carried my backpack full of materials around everywhere these days, so at least I had some enchanting material to start with.

"I'm told the information is not necessary for the successful completion of the mission."

I coughed slightly, noting the frostiness in her tone. Still, I knew better than to voice my dissatisfaction. Not at this moment anyway. We had bigger fish to fry. Anyway, I would hopefully have an answer in a few days.

As we turned the corner of the street leading to the orphanage, I let out a low hiss. No surprise there was almost no foot traffic. As a mage, I was significantly more sensitive, but the pervasive chill and the hairs that stood on my forearm were something even a mundane would pick up. Unconsciously, those who could would avoid this road, leaving the area devoid of life. Even those flying rats—pigeons that is—had left the surroundings, content to peck away at discarded refuse somewhere else.

"Can the children live somewhere else?" I asked, holding my hand outward and flushing the air in front of me with my own mana. With my Mana Sight, I could see the way my mana—a pure, clean blue—interacted with the ambient mana in the air. It slowly darkened as the chill that emanated from the orphanage actively infused the newly released energy. I stopped my little experiment and looked back at the building, noting the now-visible glow of the shorted ritual circles. No surprise that a well-made ritual circle didn't glow like a Christmas tree—or a broken one—did.

"Not long-term. If we moved them out, it'd be a flag for the state," Alexa said, crossing her arms. "The abbess is planning an impromptu 'road trip,' but it's not a long-term solution. There's too many of them."

I grunted, accepting her words. Good thing it was still good enough weather that no one was going to jump up and down if they took the kids out camping or something.

"I'll see what I can do." I got out of the car with Alexa after she parked. Together, we hurried within to locate the abbess. The woman, unlike my prejudicial and preconceived notions, was neither old and dumpy nor wrinkly and grumpy. She was, in fact, just another boomer woman in a nun's habit. Take away the habit, and I probably wouldn't have given her a second look.

"Magus Tsien," the Abbess said, inclining her head slightly. "I understand you might have a solution for us?"

"I do?" I said, then coughed. "I do. Right. So we've got two problems. The overflow into the streets and the kids."

"And the breaking seal."

"That's for later," I said, waving my hand to dismiss the abbess's words. "I'll need to do a lot more study on that, but I should be able to offer the kids something to bolster their aura. And you all too."

"The staff do not require such devices," the abbess said flatly, and I nodded. Fine. I was sure they had their own methods of dealing with it. "What do you require?"

I paused, considering my options. "Let's start by creating a warding circle in a few rooms. Maybe your cafeteria and gym? Places you can bunk the children down in and where they can congregate. It'll help in the short-term while I work out portable shields."

The abbess led me to the gym immediately. It amused me that the gym also consisted of a stage, a place where the children could put on little performances for each other, but my amusement fled quickly when I reached out with my senses to test the surroundings. Damn, there was a lot of bad mana. Even if I locked everything out, I'd need to figure out a mana scrubber of some sort. Though I guess I could let the kids' own natural resistances slowly cleanse it.

Or maybe not.

"Do you have a woodshop? Or welding equipment? I'll need solder, wood, paint, and any brushes you can gather," I said directly to the Abbess who nodded her head and strode off to get going. I turned toward Alexa next while fishing out a notepad from my backpack. "I'm going to give you a shopping list. Do me a favor and pick it up from El? And swing by the house to pick up my mortar and pestle."

Orders given, I sat in the middle of the gym and started figuring out the ritual of protection. Luckily, I knew quite a few thanks to the knowledge stuffed into my head. I just had to modify the rituals slightly to take in our surroundings and ensure it worked harmoniously. I really, really needed to work on some formation flags. Sometimes, stealing—sorry, borrowing— from other magical conventions could make my life easier, but, right now, I had to work with what I had.

Unconsciously, I continued to sample the corrupted as I worked, running the mana through my system and cleansing bits and pieces as I sat there. Corrupted mana was weird. It didn't directly injure in the short-term. It was generally a milder poison, one that affected mental and emotional states first before it harmed the body. Exact effects depended on the mana corruption itself, making individuals grumpy or tired or irate. Mild headaches were part symptom, part defense mechanism on a body and soul's part. Long-term exposure to corrupt mana on the other hand could lead to fomori, to twisted and corrupted humans, but that kind of effect took years.

The abbess arrived first and deposited my requirements. I ignored her, my hands held out before me as I slowly manipulated the spell formula only I could see. No point in making it visible, so I kept the entire thing visible only to those with the sight. However, to my surprise, I noted she was staring at the space where the formula hung, the model ritual circle slowly rotating as I flooded the construct with mana.

"Interesting. So the rumors are true. You really are not classically trained."

"Nope." I slowly clapped my hands together, dispersing the formula. It worked. Now, I just needed the materials from Alexa, and I could begin. "Did you need anything?"

"Do you have a timeline?"

"When it's done?" I shrugged my shoulders. "Placing the ritual itself should be an hour or two of work. Figure an hour of prep once Alexa is back. Then I've got to repeat it for at least one more room. In between, I'll need to work out how to contain or, better, scrub the mana the building is emanating."

The Abbess frowned. "The building?"

"Yup. The ritual circle is broken but not completely. It's like a live wire that's been stripped, shooting sparks from the stripped areas but still functioning," I said, shaking my head. "If you haven't already fired your contractors, you should do it immediately. And then hire someone actually qualified."

"We have done so," the abbess said stiffly. "Standard regulations are not to use uncertified supernatural assets, but matters have progressed."

"Great. Next, this is going to be a lot easier if you tell me what I'm trying to contain."

"That information is restricted."

"I just—"

"It is restricted even from me, Magus Tsien," the abbess said, her brows lowering. "I have no direct knowledge of what is below us."

"And indirectly?"

"Rumors. Hearsay."

"Better than nothing," I said.

"Really? If you were to take insufficient precautions because of what I said, would it be better?"

"No, but I won't make that mistake," I said softly. "So…"

"A spirit. A powerful one, not malevolent by nature," the Abbess said, waving her hand around to indicate the mana overflow. I had to agree. Cold and disturbing as it might be, it was not actively dangerous. If it had been, we'd be in a lot more trouble. "But not a friend of humanity."

"Thank you. If there's nothing else, I should work on the formula for the individual works though," I said.

The Abbess nodded, indicating she would inform me when Alexa made her way back.

Once I was left alone, I sat silent in thought, turning over the information provided to me. In the end, I dismissed it. It didn't matter, not for what I needed to do now.

***

Pendants. Those were the simplest to make. A small wooden or metal strip with enchanted spell forms within. The enchantment itself was a variation of the Force Shield spell I had, just with the entire "force" section stripped out and replaced with a modified Healing Ward. I wasn't actively trying to heal them, of course, but trigger the body's intrinsic aura, increasing its effectiveness and reinforcing it with the Shield aspect.

Unfortunately, while an individual's aura was technically part of their body and thus could be healed, my own healing spell wasn't very targeted. It did help that certain spells—like Confusion and Track—had active components within their spell formula that dealt with an aura. The former to bypass, and the latter to target. It meant I could pull relevant portions of the spell together with my Shield, Heal, and Ward options to cobble together a badly made spell.

With a gesture, I finalized the spell formula and cast it, letting the spell rotate in the air in front of me, fully visible.

Aura Shield
Synchronicity 89%
Efficiency 41%

"41%?" I muttered, staring at the glowing numbers. Given a little more time and effort, I was sure I could raise the efficiency by another 20 percent at least. I knew there was a lot of wasted power, areas I'd taken from other spells that had no place in this one.

"Exactly why do you need hob dung?" Alexa asked, dropping packages by my side.

"Part of the ritual," I replied. I took a look at the packages, sorting them quickly before I pushed the bag back toward Alexa. "Can you grind the first five ingredients together and then mix them into the paint?"

"The first five…" Alexa's eyebrows furrowed as she stared at the list in her hand. "That includes the dung."

"Unless you want me to stop carving pendants," I said, gesturing at the strip of wood that sat waiting for my first attempt.

"For the children?"

"For the children."

"I hate you."

I flashed Alexa a grin as I picked up the hot soldering iron and leaned forward toward the wood. Ah, the privileges of being the specialized help.

***

By the time I was done with my first working wooden pendant, Alexa had the paint ready.

"Put this on." I tossed the block to her underhand.

Alexa frowned, gripping the four-inch strip in hand and turning it around. "How?"

"Drill a hole, thread some string," I said, waving my hand absently as I focused on the paint. It looked like the right color. "Just don't mess up the runes. Oh, and if you can drill more holes in the wood strips, I can work around them next time."

Grumbling to herself, Alexa quickly processed the wooden strip and dropped it around her neck. She tilted her head from side to side, as if trying to hear a difference. I ignored her though, since I knew it worked. After all, I had made it. And yes, tested it.

I picked up the bucket of paint and brush, muttering the spell to myself while I considered where to start. Over the entrance doors so it had the best chance to dry, and if someone walked in on me I wouldn't lose too much work? Or start in the middle of the wall to get a nice flow going?

Decisions, decisions, decisions.

Muttering to myself, I decided on the door itself and grabbed a chair to stand on. Time to get started.

"You could use a ladder…"

"Ladder smadder."

"What does that mean?"

Meh. I ignored her, propping the chair and standing to reach for the top of the doorframe. Now, where was I? Right, creating a multi-stage, room-wide ritual to contain mana from a decades-old spirit with store-bought paint, dung, and moss.

***

Breathing was hard. My chest locked tight as I dragged on the dregs of the mana within my body. The ritual had taken more from me to charge than I had expected, the corrupted mana within the building flowing into me at a significantly lower degree than normal. It meant I could not regenerate what I had used as efficiently, draining my internal stores further. And unfortunately, I didn't have a mana battery of any sort, at least nothing I could drain myself. Stupid.

Still, as I painted the last circle and dotted it, I could feel the ritual snap into place. For a second, it stuttered as it drew upon my body for its initial charge and found my lack of mana disturbing. Rather than let the ritual fail, I bit my tongue and spat the blood directly onto the paint, watching the ritual flare back to life as it drew forth the very life essence I had gifted it. Of course, it wasn't just any blood, it was blood that had a touch of my life essence. It was the reason why blood magic wasn't something you could practice on yourself continuously. It wasn't blood in terms of scientific blood but the life essence, the portion of your soul that burned and thrived. Do it too often, and you'd basically die.

But for a short burst of fuel? Nothing like it.

"Henry?" Alexa's voice came from behind me, hesitant but concerned. I ignored it as I focused on the ritual to make sure I hadn't made a mistake. Given the boost from my blood, the ritual finally managed to draw from the corrupted ambient mana and sprang to life, a protective bubble spreading across the surfaces of the room. It locked the mana within, stopping the flow of the corrupted mana from entering.

With a thump, I sat down and put my head between my legs, breathing deeply.

"Henry?" Alexa said, more urgently now.

"Pain killers." I groaned around my knees as I tried to focus on my breathing. Right. Smaller room next time.

Dry-swallowing the pills proffered, it took me another half hour before I felt human enough to speak. By that time, the corrupted mana in the room had decreased significantly since the children who had been brought into the room slowly cleansed the mana through their own auras. As I looked around, I noted how many kids there were. And the looks they were giving me.

"Do I have two heads or something?" I muttered to myself.

Alexa, hanging close by, smiled wryly. "No, but you're a mage. And they're Templars-to-be."

"Right. We're all evil."

"It's a little more complicated than that."

"But for the kids, it works out to that, eh?" I said, crossing my arms grumpily and glaring at the kids. It made more than a few look away, though one particular redheaded young teen met my gaze fearlessly. She even wrinkled her freckled nose at me.

"Just about. How's your mana pool?" Alexa asked softly. A glance upward—which really made no sense, since it was always there—and I answered her.

"Twenty-one percent. I'm going to need to meditate."

"Okay," Alexa said simply, and I flopped straight down on the floor again. After a moment's consideration, I stood back up and hunted down a more comfortable chair while ignoring the little snickers from the kids. I was no damn Buddhist monk.

Hours later, I finished the twelfth pendant and felt a crack in my back when I stretched. I tossed the enchanted device to Alexa while I took a look at the snaking sunlight from the high windows.

"This is going too slow," I said to Alexa when she got back.

"Agreed. There's nearly fifty children, and you've only got twelve done," Alexa tapped her lips. "Suggestions?"

"Money. I can't be the only one to have come up with the idea of aura-reinforcing enchantments. If we go shopping with the d... donated money, we should be able to find something," I said. "Or you will."

"What are you going to do?" Alexa asked with a frown.

"There's a fence that needs fixing. At the least, I should see if it's possible," I said.

"Pretty sure it isn't." Alexa pointed to me. "You nearly fainted doing just this room."

I hesitated but turned away from that rather uncomfortable truth. I was sure Caleb could fix this entire thing with a wave of his hands, but the damn mage had made his view on the matter entirely too clear. As it stood, I had a slim chance of putting up a ritual large enough to block the corrupted mana. For that matter… "Crap."

"Language, Henry!"

"Sorry." I bobbed my head at the glaring pair of nuns nearby while I spotted one precocious little kid mouthing my swear word. "But I realized there's no way I'm going to be able to fix the ritual either. Not, well, not as it stands."

"Because you don't have the mana."

"Right," I said.

Alexa frowned even more at my admission, looking first at me and then around at the children. "That's not acceptable, Henry. Start thinking. I'm going to go shopping."

"It…" I shut up as I watched the blonde initiate stalk off, tension radiating from every step. After a moment, I sighed and sat on my chair, propping my head on one arm as I turned my thoughts on how to power a building-wide ritual enough to fix it and then fix the ritual below. All the while not really understanding either.

Chapter 14

"Is this going to work?" Alexa asked as she stared at my most recent experiment. I looked at the staff members of the orphanage I could see, a steel chain held in their hands as they circled the large stone building and the small, fenced-off grounds that encompassed the orphanage.

"Maybe?" I said with little confidence. "Theoretically, it should work. The chain works. I can draw the mana I need from those who grip the chain so long as they're willing, but it's a lot of mana."

"It's not dangerous, right?"

"Not majorly so," I said. "I've set up the runes to disperse the buildup if we fail. It costs more mana, but the buildup is significant enough that it makes sense."

Alexa sighed while the abbess who had been watching quietly nodded her agreement for me to continue. The abbess herself was staying out of the ring, for reasons left unexplained to me. Probably a lack of confidence in my work. I'd be insulted if I wasn't making it all up on the go. Thankfully, magic—or at least magic as I practiced it—was flexible. There might be more efficient ways of doing something, but if you had the right tools to start, you could patch things together.

In this case, it was just a much, much, much larger version of the room ritual. Except, this time around, I was containing the mana rather than letting it out. It did raise a few concerning issues, like what would happen to the continual buildup, but in the short-term, at least the neighborhood could get back to its usual state.

"Ready?" I called out. I walked forward when I received confirmation, laying a hand on the chain myself while I began the process of completing the enchantment around the fence. I was using a mixture of enchantments and empowerment on the fence. The initial enchantments had been inscribed—discretely—around the fence at intervals. I enchanted and reinforced each of those glyphs, creating anchor points for the ritual. I would then empower the remainder of the spell, giving it temporary life while we worked on fixing the source.

The enchanted-and-empowered spell was a perfect blend of strength and flexibility. Rather than draining all of us attempting to affix a permanent ritual in place, the mostly empowered ritual would give us the effects without the drain. Also, it was definitely less eye-catching since empowered runes were not visible to the naked eye.

Rune after rune layered the wall as I walked, one hand on the chain and the other outstretched to the fence. A part of me knew how weird this looked—a twenty-year-old Asian man wandering the circle of a building, hand outstretched while a bunch of nuns stood around holding a metallic chain with pained looks on their faces. I was just glad the polluted mana kept passersby out of the streets, leaving few witnesses. Of course, it only needed one with a mobile phone…

But I did what I could. And hoped everything else fell into place.

What surprised me the most was how clear and abundant the mana I drew from the staff was. While I knew they had a lot from my Mana Sight, knowing and interacting with it were entirely different things. There was also an openness to the draw, to the gifting, that I had never experienced before. I made a mental note to talk to Lily about this later as it made the entire day so much easier to work from.

In a short span of time, I completed the ritual. The final lurch of it kicking in drew mana from me and the ladies quite harshly, but with the shared draw, I found it somewhat easier to handle than the first rit. I still found myself slumped to the ground at the end, exhaustion and a headache wracking my body, but at least I wasn't spitting out blood.

"Come on, let's get you back," Alexa said softly, one hand reaching under my armpit to lift me up.

"Can't. Got to get more pendants…"

"They'll sleep in the gym for now," Alexa said, dragging me reluctantly along. "You need to rest."

"But—"

"Do you want to blow up another artifact because you were too tired?"

"It was just a few wooden blocks," I muttered disconsolately, but I did let her put me in the car. It was only when she was shaking my shoulder to wake me after we'd arrived when I realized how tired I was. With bleary eyes and a thumping headache, I didn't even make it up the stairs, instead flopping straight onto the living room couch.

***

I woke to the smell of coffee the next morning. The hiss of cooking bacon and the aroma of freshly made coffee and toasted bread had me stumbling toward the kitchen table. As I sat, I realized with a shock how hungry I truly was and attacked the toasted bread ravenously. Strawberry jam and peanut butter were slathered on with wild abandon even as a cup of coffee was thumped next to me. Only when the black hole in my stomach had faded away did I look up.

"Feeling better?" Lily asked, head propped on her shoulder. At my assent, she wrinkled her nose before she grinned and waved a hand at me. "Congratulations."

Level Up!
You are now a Level 23 Mage.
You have acquired a new spell - Cleanse
You have acquired a new spell—Increase Resistance

You have acquired a new spell—Enchanted Runes
Rituals Skill increased

"Trying a new format?" I asked, mentally dismissing the notifications. Surprisingly, my head didn't throb at all from the new knowledge, though I noted I suddenly had a slew of new information in my brain. Presumably, Lily had deposited this information while I was asleep and only just now unlocked them.

"What do you think?"

"It could do without the unicorns, rainbows, and fireworks," I said, fishing one of the pieces of bacon from what was added to the plate and then juggling it from hand to hand. "Hot, hot, hot!"

"Then wait, you idiot." Alexa rolled her eyes as she returned to the grease-laden pan to add eggs.

"What's with the breakfast? Not that I'm complaining," I said.

"Lily mentioned you'd need more energy today. After the experience and mana drain," Alexa said. "Also… thanks."

"You're welcome." I finished chewing my bacon and swallowed it. "For what?"

"Helping. You didn't need to. Especially the fence," Alexa said.

"The job's to keep them running. Having Wish orphanage close down because everyone on the block is freaking out is probably not a great idea," I said, then paused. "Huh. Or not."

"I don't like that look."

"I do," Lily said with her head propped up on her hand and a mischievous grin playing on her lips.

"Well, they've got a problem with too-high prices and people wanting them out, right? Because the neighborhood is desirable?" I said. When I got nods, I shrugged. "If we let the mana leak out…"

Alexa hummed slightly in thought and turned back toward the pan to flip the eggs. I let her think about it for a moment while I continued to stuff my face.

"No. That'd be wrong," Alexa said finally. "We can't destroy other people's livelihoods just because it's more convenient for us."

"Heee…" I said, leaning back. "Fine. So what's the plan for today?"

"Mushrooms."

I ended up making a face at her words but nodded. It'd been a few days since Corey had dropped by, which was a bit of a concern. I mean, by now, he'd have run the mana batteries out, so he should have come by to deposit our share of the mushrooms. Since he hadn't—"Where to?"

"I have his home information."

"Great," I said and then speared another piece of toast. We would get right on it. After breakfast and my lessons.

***

Autumn was always a strange time. Everything was dying, sort of, getting ready for a winter. There were leaves on the ground, brown grass everywhere, and gutters overflowing. Yet, outside of the city, the signs of life could still be seen: the occasional darting squirrel, crows and hares scampering across a highway, and a weirdness to the mana flow, an ageing to it that made casting spells that require more concentration easier. I spent most of the drive exploring that sensation, pulling at the world's mana and dispersing the accumulation after running it through basic spell constructs.

"We should be there soon," Alexa said, and I nodded. I was surprised at how far out Corey lived. Or perhaps, I shouldn't have been. Staying next to a national park meant easy access to the woods, where herbs and other supernatural materials might be found. Alexa had picked me up right after I finished with Caleb, which meant we'd been able to skip rush-hour traffic for the most part. Still, the entire drive had taken a couple hours.

"Great." I shifted in my chair once more and dispersed the mana I held, absently checking my body for how much I was at. It was probably around 80 percent of my full, though that new full level I knew had once again increased. A quick check against my mana bar showed I was right, which made me smirk.

A turn and we were off the country road and entering a small side road. Within seconds, a large residential building appeared before our eyes. If it was a little more opulent and a little less rundown and practical, it could have been called a mansion. As it stood, it just looked like a very large, practical building. Perhaps even more surprising were the numerous plots of farmed land, each of which were separated by ramshackle fencing. I peered at the plants within, vaguely thinking I knew some of them, but I decided not to push it. After all, I knew my limits, and herbology was definitely one of them.

Perhaps just as surprising were the large number of individuals moving around the plot of land. There were at least a dozen kids rushing around, naked as the day they were born. Four feet tall and thin and grey, the mini-trolls acted just like human kids. Well, except for the one who was eating a centipede raw. As interesting were the four trolls, three women and a young male, who were working the fields, weeding, watering, and turning over the ground. When we pulled up, they stared until we exited the vehicle.

"Hi there," I said, raising my hand and offering them a smile.

"This is private property. Didn't you read the sign?" An older troll female walked up. I squinted slightly, letting the glamour she used come into focus and noted the middle-aged brunette who came into focus before I let my gaze sharpen again.

"We did, but we're actually looking for Corey," I said. A younger female troll's face twisted at the mention of Corey's name, concern quickly buried. Or at least, I hoped it was concern.

"He's not here. Please leave."

"Do you know where he might be?" I asked, pushing my luck.

"We don't know. We'll let him know you're looking for him when he's back," the matron said again.

"You don't even know who we are," I said, crossing my arms. "And he can't be harvesting any more mushrooms without more mana batteries."

"You're the mage?" The matron's tone went from coolly polite to completely unfriendly in a flash. She crossed her arms even as the younger female suddenly looked full of hope. "Leave then, Mage. You should know the courtesies required. You have been requested to leave numerous times already."

I found myself growling slightly at her words, leaning forward as I realized something was being hidden. Before I could say anything further, Alexa spoke up.

"Our apologies. We were but concerned. We'll leave now," she said. Without a further word, she got into the car and turned the engine on, leaving me staring at her. The initiate waved for me to step in when I looked at her, forcing me to choose between being abandoned or getting more information.

"What was all that about?" I growled when I sat inside.

"Courtesies and rules. We're in their home. If we continue to push things, we'll ruin our reputation," Alexa said.

I snarled. "They know something."

"They do, but if we stay after being requested to leave so bluntly, it'd be tantamount to declaring war with them. Then where would we be?" Alexa said with a snort.

"Fine…" I crossed my arms, understanding her point if not particularly impressed with the results. "How are we going to find him now?"

Alexa smiled slightly and pointed to the glove compartment as she slowly backed us away from the house. Inside, I found a small vial, one that contained a dark-red, viscous liquid.

"That's blood," I said with a frown. "Corey's?"

"Yes. Unlike you, I never trusted the troll to keep his word without some insurance," Alexa said simply. "Are you able to track him?"

I frowned again, extending my senses within the blood. It was old, though the preservation runes set around the vial had slowed its degradation. Corey's aura was still captured within, though within a few days, it'd be gone completely. I wonder what Alexa would have done then? Possibly just gotten another vial. I wanted to berate her for taking someone's blood as insurance, considering how dangerous something like this could be in the wrong hands. Then again, here we were, using it. And realistically, the amount taken was so low, it would be difficult to cast a really dangerous spell.

"Yes," I said. "Give me a few minutes. It's weak."

Alexa nodded, having the car in idle at the entrance to the road from the turnoff. I eyed our surroundings again before I fished in my backpack for the compass and drew a deep breath, getting ready to track our missing troll.

***

An hour later, we were rolling down a worn, potted country road. The singular sign indicating it was Private Property was hanging askew from a single, rusted nail. Obviously, between that, the road, and the peeling paint, it was clear the farm we were now traveling toward had been abandoned for some time. It still amazed me that buildings, especially ones so close to town, could be so easily be abandoned. Perhaps it said something of the sad state of humanity and our society that there'd be dozens of people on the streets and even more abandoned, discarded buildings like this within miles of each other.

"What do you think he'd be doing here?" I muttered, staring at the abandoned farm. Obviously, we weren't the only trespassers here in the last few years, though I had no intention of leaving my mark. I never did get the point of casual graffiti, not emotionally at least. Even if someone did want to leave a sign of their passing, they should at least do so in a manner that actually informed others of who they were because C.M. could be anyone.

"Probably looking for herbs," Alexa said, eyeing the broken windows and the single, fluttering curtain. "House or barn first?"

"Neither," I said as I glanced at the compass. It had shifted since we drew close, able to provide slightly better guidance, and was now pointing unerringly toward the small copse of trees behind the buildings. Once I explained the matter, Alexa pulled the car over and set up her spear. I, on the other hand, jittered, debating taking my backpack and loading it with more survival gear or not. In the end, I stuffed in more bottles of water, an emergency blanket, and some extra food. At Alexa's half smile at my antics, I explained. "Mages are prepared for anything."

"So are scouts, but we're not staying the night," Alexa said. "If it's longer than an hour, we go back."

"But—"

"I'm not wasting more than a day on a troll," Alexa said forcefully. "We still have a ritual that's breaking to deal with."

"He has a family who is waiting for him!" I protested.

"His wives will make do. His son looks about old enough to take on the responsibilities of the family anyway," Alexa countered as she headed into the forest. I fell into step with her, occasionally glancing at the compass and the ground. Not that I could track a herd of elephants through a glass store, but a man could hope.

"Wait. Wives?"

"Yes, didn't you see them?" Alexa turned to glance at me. "Don't tell me you mistook them for males. They're not that different."

"No, I knew they were women," I said. "And none of the stories ever mentioned female satyrs!"

"Uh huh," Alexa said.

"But wives?" I muttered, thinking about it. Well, I guess it made sense. Sort of. I mean, humans had multiple-wife cultures, so why shouldn't monsters? For that matter, I shouldn't be surprised if monsters didn't even get married. They were, literally, monsters. Though supes might be a better term, since they weren't actually monsters. Ugh. My head hurt sometimes figuring out terminology.

Alexa ignored my mutterings, focused as she was on our trek within the forest. Thankfully, there seemed to be an often-used deer track here, which we presumed had been used by Corey too. In either case, at one point, Alexa even stopped to point out a relatively clear footprint embedded in dried mud.

"It rained, what, last night?" I inquired out loud and got a nod from Alexa. With some indication we were on the right track, the pair of us sped up.

Forty minutes later, slightly out of breath, Alexa raised her hand and stopped me from stepping into the clearing. I frowned, the fading light of day making it hard to see within the forest. "What?"

"Light Ball, inside the clearing please," Alexa said simply, her spear casually leveled toward it. Rather than ask why, I muttered the words for the spell and made a Light Ball blossom within, pumping a small amount of mana in it but keeping a tether to it just in case.

Light Ball Cast
Synchronicity 94%
Efficiency 82%

The light blossomed, shedding a gentle yellow light that filled the clearing and cast back shadows. As the light reached upward, my gaze was attracted to minor movement that set leaves shivering and branches bouncing.

"Whaaat?"

"Shhhhh," Alexa hissed and then took a step backward. When she realized I hadn't followed her lead, she hissed. "Back."

"But—"

"Giant spiders," Alexa said softly. "If he's been caught, he's dead."

"That's not right," I said but followed her lead, backing off. I proceeded to pre-cast Fireball in my mind, building up the spell formulas while I had time. "In Lord of the Rings—"

"Not a book," Alexa said, cutting me off. "And Corey's not a full-blood troll. His regeneration is probably only twice or thrice as efficient as yours. He's dead. Or so close, he might as well be."

"You can't know that," I said, coming to a stop and growling softly. The Fireball formed in my mind, ready to be used, while I tied off the Light Ball and began dual-casting a Force Spear.

"No. I can't. But I'm not risking our lives for a dead troll," Alexa said.

"But…" I paused, then realized something. "He's alive. He has to be, or else his blood wouldn't be working as strongly."

My words made Alexa pause for a second before she shook her head, waving me backward. "Doesn't matter. He's not our responsibility."

"It's our fault he was looking for those mushrooms," I said, spreading my feet. "And I don't understand why you're refusing to help."

"Because he's a troll," Alexa hissed while scanning the treetops around us, her spear held in both hands.

"Who's got wives and kids. A family," I said. "Who worked for us, talked to us. Hell, even shared his snacks with us."

"Lower your voice!" Alexa snarled softly.

"Yes, do shut up!"

"I won't—" I paused, my brain catching up finally. Eyes wide, I turned toward where the third voice had erupted from and blinked. "Corey?"

"Yes. While it was nice to hear you defending me, your friend is right. We should go," Corey said, limping out from the undergrowth where the camo-clad troll with his grey skin was easier to see. I absently noted he had a bag hanging from his shoulder.

"Incoming!" Alexa snarled and side-stepped suddenly, allowing the dropping spider to miss her and fall to hang between the two of us. While she did so, she struck out and stabbed a second spider. On instinct, I released my first held spell, the Fireball smashing into the large spider and burning through its skin, sending it shaking and twisting in the air. With an abrupt, strangled shriek/squeak, it dropped the rest of the way to the ground even as its body burned from within.

"Die!" I snarled and football-kicked the small-dog-sized spider away. In passing, I absently noted the monster had red spots on its back and big, big fangs. Fangs? No, different word. I didn't have time to care. As it skidded among the dry leaves, creating a mini-tsunami of discarded vegetation, I followed up my attack with my Force Spear, pinning and killing the creature.

"Time to go!" Alexa said, having extracted her spear and now using it as a bat. As the loud, skittering noises and the rustling of the branches increased, I started backing off at speed, Force Balls conjuring beside me. As spiders dropped toward us, I fired my spell effects at the large arachnids, battering them away.

Of course, the only negative of that was since they were falling on their threads, physics eventually had its way and swung the damn monsters back toward us. After the second swinging spider nearly took me in the chest, I really sped moving backward. Thankfully, the spiders weren't willing to follow us too far from their nest. Either that or the accumulated losses from Alexa's and my repeated attacks finally made them give up.

"Where's Corey?" I asked after we had backed off another twenty feet from the point where we last saw the spiders stop. I received a shrug in reply from Alexa, and my eyes narrowed. A quick fumble and check and I realized the needle was now pointing back the way we came.

When we finally made it back to the car, we found Corey leaning against it, a cigarette between his lips.

"You left us!" I said, waving my hands.

"I did," Corey admitted unashamedly.

"We came looking for you!" I said heatedly.

"And it was real nice." Corey nodded. "But I didn't ask you to. And it wasn't me who was busy attracting the spiders. If you'd been quiet, I would have been able to sneak back out."

"Sneak?"

Corey nodded, patting his bag. "Blood blossom spider eggs. Worth a pretty penny, but their parents are very territorial. Took me days to get in and out."

While I fumed, Alexa pointed at the bag, her voice cool. "And the mushrooms?"

"Got them too. Four more. You want to take them here or for me to drop them off at your place?"

"We'll take them here," Alexa said, and Corey nodded, pulling the bag off his shoulder.

As he rummaged within, he continued. "Going to need another set of batteries. Pulled the ones you gave me out while I was working, but I'm down to one recharge."

I growled and jerked slightly, but Alexa tugged on the backpack over my shoulders. I reluctantly gave it up and watched as Alexa fished the mana batteries out, receiving the Wynn mushrooms as well as the now-defunct batteries from the troll. After confirming our next appointment, we left, leaving the troll to head back home by himself. A part of me—the nice, polite part—wanted to offer the troll a ride back. However, the grumpy, hurt, and bewildered portion won, and I stayed silent till we were back on the highway.

"How can you be so, so, blasé about that?" I asked with a slight snarl.

"He was right. He didn't ask us to rescue him," Alexa said with a shrug. "And he still got us another four mushrooms."

"But he left us to die!"

"Don't be so melodramatic. It was just a nest of blood blossom spiders. At worst, you could have burned the trees and really scared them off," Alexa said, lips parting. "Of course, I'm glad we didn't start a forest fire, but we were never really in danger."

"But—"

"Henry," Alexa said, using my name to catch my attention as she drove. "He's a troll. You're a mage. I'm a Templar. We have a nice, simple business arrangement. Stop trying to make it more than it is."

"Why'd you even agree to go looking for him if you didn't give a damn?" I asked.

"He has your compass and mana-battery system," Alexa said. "It's not exactly impossible for him to find someone else to recharge the batteries, is it?"

"No," I admitted and then frowned at the Templar. "So, that's it? You decided to follow up to make sure we got my gear back?"

"And take any mushrooms he had collected. And the breakage fee for the contract," Alexa added.

I crossed my arms and growled slightly, glaring at Alexa as my irritation grew. Gah. These, these… supes. They were all callous, annoying idiots. Business deal. I growled, falling silent as Lily's reminder resounded in my mind. As much as I sometimes thought I knew Alexa, I also had a tendency to forget that the same woman who snored in her sleep and had to be taught what Cowboy Bebop was was also a cold-blooded killer of supernaturals.

Perhaps… perhaps helping her complete her quest might not be the best idea there was. Lost in thought, I fell silent as we drove the rest of the way home.

Chapter 15

"You seem troubled today," Caleb said to me after my latest ritual attempt fizzled out, breaking at a baker's dozen of points. I prodded at the spell formulas, irritation coursing through me as I realized I had literally just looked at these lines.

"I'm fine," I said.

"No. You're in the twenty-third dimension, the elemental plane of metal and Kuala Lumpur," Caleb said, tapping the ritual. "Or your summon would be at least. And maybe portions in Johannesburg."

"Fine." I leaned back and crossed my arms while staring at the older mage. He returned my glare calmly until I broke. "I had an argument with Alexa."

"If this is a relationship issue, you may leave now," Caleb said.

"Of course not!" I said. "It's just, she treats the supernaturals like they're not, you know, human. And I can't help but think, well, does she think of me like that? Should I be helping her?"

"And you believe supernaturals to be human like you," Caleb said simply.

"Well, not exactly like me," I said slowly. "But the races, they're sentient. Good."

"Some. Some are very similar to us. Others have strange beliefs and rituals, biology that requires different things. The vampires and their need for blood, lycanthropes who lock themselves away every twenty-eight days, the ghouls who must eat corpses to survive," Caleb said. "The Templars have good reason to treat each race coldly. There is a long history of each race preying upon humanity."

"But they're not doing that now," I said stubbornly.

"True. Modern society and overpopulation have allowed many races to live in relative peace with humanity. Resources are significantly more abundant," Caleb said. "But even if as a percentage the number of malcontents has dropped, the increase in all populations has seen a total increase in attacks. Add the slowly decreasing number of Templars as years of continued secrecy take their toll, and you begin to see how they have taken a harder line."

"But she wasn't like that earlier!" I said, crossing my hands.

"Really?"

I opened my mouth to retort but closed it, and my brain began the slow process of evaluating all the things Alexa had ever done. We'd worked a ton of quests together, but I recalled how she almost always pushed for the harder ones, the extermination quests. Almost always monsters, almost always creatures who were, without a doubt, something that needed killing. Even when we took on more mundane tasks, she never really interacted socially with our employers. Oh, she was cordial and polite, but she never tried to find out about their lives, never asked how they were doing.

"Huh."

"You object to Ms. Dumough's attitude, but have you considered that your own might be a product of your advantages?" Caleb said.

"My advantages?" I asked.

"Unlike most, you are protected." Caleb pointed to the ring on my finger, the object of magical import. "You cannot make a mistake that will see your instantaneous death. Creatures of true power are barred from attacking you, leaving you to contend with only the lowest, and those offer you the respect and wariness that is your due as a mage. Few would turn away a closer relationship with a powerful mage."

"You're saying they're friendly because I could be useful?" I asked, somewhat hurt by the implication. I wasn't exactly Mr. Popular at school, being Asian and a nerd, but I wasn't exactly unpopular either. I just had my own friends. I thought it was just a case of finding more people who were like me, like a giant convention.

"Somewhat," Caleb said. "Your power is useful, but Ms. Dumough on the other hand represents a power that has hunted and will hunt them down. Offering a business arrangement, an impersonal mien, while dealing with supernatural races allows all parties to grasp and operate on a comfortable footing."

"So she might want to be friends but doesn't know how?" I asked slowly.

"I will not speculate on her feelings, but she has good reason to be wary of the races," Caleb said. "And they, of her. As would you."

"Yeah, yeah," I grumbled. That I knew. It wasn't as if I hadn't been warned that at the end of the day, my "friend" was going to demand my ring at some point, which left me wondering, once again, if I should perhaps not help her. But I knew too the Templars would just replace her, probably with someone else, someone who might not be "fated" to be here but who was less friendly.

And in the end, I did consider Alexa my friend. Even if she didn't, me.

"If we are done, let us review the ritual you have been working on," Caleb said, tapping the table to bring my attention back to him. I sighed but nodded, focusing on the ritual. It wasn't going to draw itself.

***

Later that day, I stumbled back into our house, notebook filled with scribbled notes about the ritual and other aspects of rituals. Lunch was a hurried affair, Alexa almost dragging me off my seat as I finished my noodles.

"Okay already. I'm coming," I grumped at her, shrugging my coat on and grabbing my trusty backpack. "It's not as if the ritual is going to break right this second."

"But the contractors are arriving today," Alexa said, "and they want to speak with you."

"Contractors?"

"The supernatural ones you insisted we hire," Alexa said, ushering me into the car. Within seconds, she had pulled away from the curb and merged with traffic, her fingers drumming on the steering wheel.

"Oh, those. Glad you all finally decided to be smart about it," I said, smiling grimly. With the right group, the orphanage could probably finish the necessary work without disturbing the ritual further or, at the very least, mask it so it looked like the work was done while other, more magical means were used to create the same effect.

"It is not smart to let the…" Alexa trailed off and shut her mouth.

"The what?" I asked, prodding.

"The enemy." Alexa jutted her chin out, fingers squeezing the wheel tighter as she waited for me to explode. "Wait."

I watched all this quietly but decided not to comment, the information and her reaction no longer a surprise. Though, I had a feeling her reactions were not so much over her feelings but concern over me attacking her beliefs again.

"Who do we have coming?" I asked.

"There are meant to be three contractors." Alexa's shoulders relaxed slightly at my topic change. "The Grimwalls are bidding, as are the McClintocks and PMC."

The Grimwalls were a dwarven company, one we had actually done work for before. Good people, though I was somewhat hesitant about their level of magical knowledge. After all, the last time they ran into an unusual ward, they'd hired me to figure it out.

"The McClintocks are a group of Scottish fae. They don't do a lot of work for non-fae, but since our building is mostly stone and mortar, they are willing to give it a shot. As for the PMC, they're a multi-national corporation. We'd actually tried to hire them at first, but they had no crews available. Now, they want to assess the work before committing," Alexa explained, giving me details of the two I didn't know.

"And I'm there for…"

"To reassure them the ritual is not active, to answer questions about the rituals you created, and be our magical consultant," Alexa said.

"Har. Consultants get paid," I grumbled.

"You are," Alexa pointed out, and I shut my mouth, recalling the fact that I actually did negotiate payment earlier on. I'd actually forgotten, having delegated this entire quest under "helping a friend." Since it was an actual quest, a real job, perhaps I should stop contemplating stopping work. It'd be really unprofessional after all.

When we finally pulled up, it was to the sight of the Grimwalls stomping out, the titular-named leader literally scurrying out of the building. By the time Alexa had the car parked and I was out, the dwarves were too far for me to call to them, especially considering they seemed to be very clear in their desire to be gone.

"That's not foreboding at all," I muttered. I grabbed my bag and walked in. The abbess gave me a relieved smile when she noted my presence and quickly waved me in. "Problem?"

"The atmosphere was a bit much for the Grimwalls," she said softly, gesturing within. I nodded slowly, making a face, and took directions to find the other pair of contractors in the basement, staring at some damaged wallboards. As I walked, I sampled the increased mana corruption, the dense block of corrupted mana filling the entire building and its grounds. Obviously, our attempts at containing the corruption had worked.

Legends had the fae as beautiful, amazing creatures whose very presence could enchant and terrorize in equal measure, but it was a bit of a lie really. At least for those fae who still lived on Earth. With the ever-increasing volume of iron and the corruption and destruction of nature, pure-blooded fae had left our world long ago. Only the changelings, the thin bloods, and the lower fae were left, groups who could handle the pervasive use of technology. The fae still weren't happy with their new situation, many electing to stay in communes or in smaller towns, but they stayed.

Truth be told, staring at the duo of thin bloods, I couldn't help but feel disappointed. I literally could have taken either one, dumped them in the middle of a country music concert, blinked, and have lost them.

The PMCs were somewhat more interesting. Their leader was tall and angular, his face covered by large aviator sunglasses which did little to hide his antenna or the bulge beneath the back of his coat where his wings hid. His female assistant was wearing a tank top, one leg cocked and giving the fae boys a wide grin, a red cap jauntily pressed over her long, furred ears.

"Hi there," I said, greeting everyone. Once introductions were complete, the questions started flying. It was nice to be the center of attention, especially over something I had some expertise in. It was a great ego boost, until the fae started asking questions I couldn't answer.

"No, I don't know what the eighty-third line does yet."

"You're right. That isn't a bleed-off. On second thought, it's probably Jamal's self-reinforcing transformation equation."

"I don't know if it could be bypassed. That'd depend on the inner circle which I haven't studied yet," I said finally, throwing my hands up in exasperation. I received glares from the fae at my actions, but hell. "Look, we just need you to finish the job. I'll fix the ritual eventually, but it's huge!"

"We are asking because we are not able to provide an adequate quote without sufficient information," the leading fae said, arms crossed. "You say the ritual circle is not dangerous, but you then admit you do not even understand it properly."

"Just because I don't understand what the circle is doing in its entirety doesn't mean I can't tell if it's dangerous or not," I snapped.

"Then are you willing to place your word on this?" the mothman asked, jumping in immediately.

"Yes!" I said, feet tapping with impatience. The moment I uttered my assurance, the tension in the room dissipated. I frowned, looking between the pair of consultant groups before my arm was gently yanked backward, and I was led out by an apologizing initiate.

"What?" I asked her.

"We've talked about giving your word!" Alexa said with a hiss.

"And I'll stand by this," I said and pointed at the ritual carvings around us. "Those are fine. Can't say much about the inner ritual, but so long as they avoid it, like I told them to…" I raised my voice at the last bit, making sure the contractors heard it. "We should be fine."

"Theoretically. As far as you know," Alexa pointed out.

"That's all I can offer."

"And if you're wrong, your reputation will suffer," Alexa said.

"If I'm wrong, and this place blows up, a lot more than my reputation is going to be a problem," I said, shaking my head. "No. I'll stand by my words. And if I'm wrong, I'll take the hit. But, on that note, I should be going over those rituals more. Unless you think they need me to hold their hand more?"

Alexa snorted at my words but waved me away. I took off, checking my mental map to verify the last spot I had been at as I extended my senses to encompass the slowly leaking ritual circles. Now that I was in the basement, I could sense the cold, dark mana that escaped was escaping at an even higher rate. I stared down the hallway toward the room that had been locked, my mind turning over the implications. An inadvertent side effect or an attack?

Unfortunately, I had nothing to go on, and so I turned to the external ritual, noting the areas that had been damaged and the increasingly worn areas. The initial damage was minimal, but as time passed, the ritual continued to wear itself down as the broken parts placed greater strain on the rest of the circle. In time, the entire ritual would fail.

Which was fine in itself. As I'd told the contractors, there was no chance of the external ritual blowing up. It was just a giant collector, one that focused and drew mana from the surroundings with some minor glamour and reinforcing glyphs. Part of the trick when we had created our own ritual around the fence had been in creating a one-way porous shield such that mana could still be gathered by this external ritual.

The problem was, once the external ritual failed, it would no longer power the internal, smaller containment ritual, which was the concern. Realistically, I had two choices: fix the external ritual or, failing that, modify the internal one so it did not need an external ritual. Neither was particularly easy.

Which is what brought me here, taking down notes, activating portions of the ritual so I could study the ritual formulas and then move on to the next portion.

***

Two days later, I stood before the last ritual center in contemplative silence. In my mind's eye, the ritual formulas danced, equations shifting as I adjusted the formula to patch in my fix. Eventually, I exhaled and pulled my notebook out of my pocket, canceling the latest scribbled section and writing in the new correction. With this, I should be done.

I blinked when I stepped into the sunlight a few minutes later, wincing at the harsh light hurting my eyes. Damn, I'd been down there for too long. Again.

"Are you taking a break?" the abbess asked, appearing by my shoulder like a ghost.

"No. I'm done," I said, offering her a smile.

"Done?" The excitement in her voice was palatable. "Will you be doing the ritual today?"

"No. There's a few things we need to collect," I said. Before she could ask, I pulled my notebook out of my pocket, tore the page off, and handed it to her. "The list of materials I require are here."

"We'll get it…" The abbess trailed off as she stared at the list, her jaw working silently at first before her shock finally wore off. "Isn't this a little excessive?"

"No."

"But silver dust? Eight pounds of salt, that's easy enough. Wood shavings from a two-hundred-year-old elm tree, that's—"

"It's all necessary," I said, cutting her off, my face grim. "There are three ways to strengthen and fix your ritual circle. The first is to have me do it using the materials I've requested. The second, you hire a full mage, one who has more experience and a much deeper mana pool. They'll be able to inlay the ritual formulas directly without using as many supporting materials. Or thirdly, you can find whoever put the ritual in place in the first place and have them do it.

"But I doubt the third option is viable because otherwise you'd have already taken it, and considering most mages won't work for you, the second option might not be possible either. Certainly not in the timeframe you need."

I watched as her lips pressed firmly together while my tirade continued, but I was tired, grumpy, and fed-up with having information withheld from me while being expected to make miracles happen. Perhaps there were cheaper, easier ways of completing the ritual, but we neither had the time nor did I have the inclination to consider them any longer.

"How long do you need?" I asked.

The abbess glanced at the list again and shook her head after a short while. "I do not know. Much of the material is not rare, but it is not as if we purchase these items regularly."

"Tomorrow. Or the day after. Any longer than that, and I can't promise you the inner circle will hold."

"That soon?" she asked with a hiss.

"Yes." I might be exaggerating, but I figured overestimating the wear was better than underestimating it.

"We'll get right on it."

I nodded to her, offering her a quick wave of my hand. Before I left, I checked in on the contractors—PMC being the eventual winner—in case they had any further questions. They had a few, but thankfully, unlike the mundanes, they had a clear idea of what they should or should not do. If nothing else, they just avoided the areas that were mana infused.

After that, I spent a few minutes and verified the enchantment around the gym still held before I made a couple more pendants for the kids and eventually left. It wasn't perfect, and I really hoped to clear the issue up sooner rather than later—if nothing else than to let the children make their way back to their beds at night.

It was when I was nearly home that I recalled my appointment with Adom. When I finally made it to the library, I found the figure seated at the same table we had first met, a large folder sitting across from him. I frowned, staring at the folder, but fished out the newly withdrawn payment and handed it to the supe. As I scooped up the folder, I paused.

"Is there anything I should know?"

"Of import?" Adom paused, considering. "Much of interest. Little of direct relevance to your concern. I was able to ascertain that the building had seen major renovations in the late seventies, focused on the basement area. It was marked as an extension and introduction of heating, but I understand the plans submitted were more extensive," Adom said. "However, there are no other significant notes. No burial grounds, no ley lines or previous owners of the demonic nature."

"Great!" I said with a smile and then hurried out, exhaustion wracking my body. A part of me wondered if paying that thousand dollars, money that was much needed to get exactly zero real information was worth it. Then again, perhaps it was like insurance. You hated paying for it until that one time when it panned out. Though, considering the worst case scenarios involved, I'm leaning towards never getting a payout.

Once I was finally done with delaying, I made my way home to collapse in my bed. Two long days of studying ritual formulas meant that when I did fall asleep, I dreamed of floating spell equations and a tag-team matchup of disgruntled authority figures of Caleb and the abbess taking turns berating me for my lack of talent.

Chapter 16

"No class this morning?" Lily asked, noting how slowly and languidly I was eating my breakfast.

I sipped at my coffee before I finally answered the jinn, trying desperately to banish the last of Hypnos's dust. Wait. Did Hypnos actually exist in this world? I frowned, tapping the mug of coffee in my hand with one finger. If vampires, werewolves, and the fae existed, why not gods? And if so, how the hell do I keep off their radar.

"Henry?"

"Sorry. Are gods real?" I asked.

"Real enough," Lily said. "Though they're less godlike and just beings of incredible power. Some have limits on what they can do. Others are somewhat less constrained but more… remote. The goings-on of earth and its mortals are of little concern."

"Ah…" I filed the information away before cocking my head to the side. "And no, no class today. I texted Caleb last night. I don't think I can stand another day of having ritual knowledge stuffed in my brain."

"So what are your plans for today? I notice Alexa left early."

"I understand she's helping with locating the required materials," I said. "And my plans are to turn into a giant vegetable. I still have to catch up on my reading." I pointed to the box of books that had yet to be unpacked in the corner, one labeled "unread."

"Nope," Lily said, shaking her head. "Can't do it."

"What do you mean?" I frowned. "I'm pretty sure I can."

"Nope. You've got a quest," Lily said and waved her hand.

Feed the Children

Newborn knockers require specialized sustenance. Help a mother feed her children!

"Alexa's not here…" I said, frowning at the quest information, curious to see what those damn Welsh supernaturals looked like. Certainly I'd been caught out by pop-culture expectations of what the supernaturals should be like more than once.

"Do you need her to hold your hand?" Lily asked, putting her fists on her hips. "Or are you man enough to run a little non-combat quest yourself?"

"One. That's not going to work on me. Two. I didn't accept that quest."

"Mandatory quest. You're being railroaded," Lily said with a smirk. When I refused to move my butt, she added a plaintive whine. "Please? I really want to get out of the house."

"You can always come along. Or hell, leave yourself!"

"But it's no fun without you. Please?" Lily said, putting her hands together and doing the entire big-eyes thing. Her act broke my brain for a second, the sight of an all-powerful jinn giving me wide eyes like an anime character just a little too strange.

"Enough already," I said. "I'll do it, and you can come."

"Yay!" Lily said with a wide grin. "Now, I've got to figure out what to wear." The next second, the jinn was walking to the bathroom to use the full-length mirror and her abilities to alter her clothing.

I sighed, watching her leave, and kept my thoughts and sudden realization to myself. Better to not let the all-powerful GM of my life know I saw through her naïve act, that her sudden interest in clothing was just a cover for her nervousness about going out. In truth, I was somewhat happy to see her take the initiative. While her agoraphobia had lessened significantly, Lily still did not take advantage of her freedom as much as she could. Sometimes, I wondered if it was because she was afraid it would all be taken away, snatched from her grasp by my death.

"Could have waited till I finished breakfast though," I muttered and turned back to my toast. Breakfast. Yummm…

****

Standing by the bus stop, waiting for our conveyance to arrive, I found myself staring at Lily who was seated under the supplied awning, hands clasped in front of her tightly. In her stylish, short leather coat, grey tights, and green blouse, she could have passed for any young worker on her day off.

"So, spriggans," I said, to break the silence.

"Spriggans. We've got to get their newborn food, specifically scapolite, but it can't just be any, since the purity and rarity makes a difference. It dictates the amount of mana and thus the child's growth in the beginning," Lily said. "Which is why you're here."

"Because I can see mana," I said, nodding. "Are we, or are we not going mining?"

Lily snorted, shaking her head. "Of course not. Do you think I'd dress up like this to go mining?" Lily smirked. "We're going shopping."

"Shop—" Oh. Right. There were people who actually bought rocks for amusement and health. I mentally smacked myself upside the back of my head though. Just because I used to think buying rocks because it was good energy was wasteful did not make it wrong. These days, well, I couldn't really discount anything. Being open minded was tiring damn it.

"Midtown Mall, here we go!" Lily said, waving her hand around. I laughed at her sudden exuberance and leaned in, settling down for the long wait. Right. Time to get some baby supernaturals some nice, crunchy rocks to eat.

Hours later when we finally stumbled out of the rock shop clutching our three purchases, each of which glowed with the subtle lines of condensed mana, I noted how Lily's initial excitement had waned. In fact, if not for her darker complexion, she'd have been unhealthily pale. As it stood, there was a glazed look to her eyes that I did not like. When I guided her to take a seat in the food court without protest, I knew there was something wrong.

"Here," I said, dropping a giant cup of frozen, mushed fruits in front of her. "Drink up."

"Thank you," Lily said, sipping delicately at the drink while her hands wrapped around the cup. I sat beside her, staying silent while waiting for her to get around to speaking to me. "It's just… This looked fun, you know? On your TV."

"But it isn't?" I asked, glancing around the crowd. It was the middle of the week, so the shopping mall was not, by any reasonable standards, crowded. Since this entire mall catered to the more esoteric tastes, including a couple of fortune tellers and a martial arts gym promising to teach you the "real ninjutsu," it probably was never that busy even on weekends.

"It's okay, but…" Lily exhaled. "It's been so long since I have been allowed out, and the world, your world, is so confusing. The clothing, the fashions, the language. Magic lets me understand, to grasp the changes, but it doesn't make it any less surprising."

I sipped at my drink as I waited for Lily to continue to talk while she explained what it was that was bothering her. Even if I did have an urge to perhaps offer some suggestions, I squashed it. What could I offer a millennia-old jinn? What did I know of her experiences, of her world? Sure, she had thousands of years of history to draw upon, but so many of those years she'd spent in her ring.

"It's just a change," Lily said, turning her head to look around. "But a good one. Your food, your technology is a marvel. Magic, without mana. Magic for the common people."

I smiled slightly, following her gaze to review the fast food court. Greek food, burgers, pizza, western Chinese food, burritos, juice smashed up and frozen… and people, people everywhere reading, listening to music, watching shows on their phones and tablets. Magic, in their hands.

"It is kind of amazing, isn't it? Though I still like my magic better," I said. Real magic. Except, the more I studied it, the more I realized it too had its own rules, its own restrictions. And once again, I felt a wash of gratitude that I had met Lily. Not just for making me a mage but because of the information she had downloaded to me. Like science, every aspect of the spells was built upon the works of those before. Each spell formula had been refined by hundreds, sometimes thousands of others. At my beck and call were the formulas that master mages had produced, concepts they had refined.

Of course, there was a negative to that. In many cases, I was a monkey with Lego blocks of spell formulas. Given enough time, I could kludge something together, but the blocks weren't mine, weren't optimized. Hell, sometimes I didn't even understand the blocks beyond the barest aspects. If not for the fact that Lily was slowly feeding the simplest works to me as well as my study under Caleb, I really would be no more than a monkey bashing bricks together.

"Aye, magic is amazing," Lily said and then touched her phone. "But what you've done, the stories you've created, the technology you've created could rival a god's. I should know. I've met more than a few." I chuckled, and Lily grinned back at me. "Thank you. For letting me out with your wish. I'll always remember it."

I sipped on my drink again, ducking my head at her sincere thanks. Seeing my embarrassment, Lily smirked slightly before prodding my arm. "Now. Food!"

"We just ate… Okay, fine. Lunch."

Chuckling softly, I stood and walked toward the food options. I knew better than to ask what. Her answer would just be "everything." But as I walked away, I had to admit this was a better day than my own planned one. A quest to help others, time with a friend, and physical exercise too. What more could I ask for?

Chapter 17

As I stared at the array of stern-faced nuns before me, I had a brief moment of déjà vu. One so strong, I felt disassociated for a second, like a boat tossing on the tumultuous waves of memory. Then, reality snapped back, and I gestured at the chain we'd laid along the hallways.

"We have enough?" I asked, weariness inching into my voice. After all, we'd had to run to the hardware store twice already just to get the damn thing.

"We do now," one of the nuns said waspishly.

I ignored her tone of voice and reached out to touch the chain, sending a pulse of mana down it. I followed it as it flowed, my frown deepening as I felt the whirls and whorls, the unrefined edges where spell formulas had been compressed together or hastily completed, leaving a leakage. By the time the mana pulse had made its way back to me, it had lost nearly eighty percent of its charge. Unacceptable if I had more time. Utterly unacceptable.

But…

"All right, get to your positions," I said, dropping the chain and waving the nuns aside. I turned away from the group as they moved away, my mind focused on the other, bigger problem. In minutes, I was before the inner ritual circle room, my hand raised to test its integrity.

Bad. Even without extending my senses, I felt the psychic wind of mana blowing, the pressure being exerted by the being that was contained within the ritual. It was hidden, locked away in another dimension, but through the cracks, through the failing of the ritual circle, it was getting stronger. Much, much stronger. It felt—

"What is it?" Alexa asked when she caught me standing there, my hand extended and a frown on my face.

"Nothing."

"What is it," Alexa demanded.

"It feels like whoever—whatever is behind the circle, it's pushing with everything it's got. It's sacrificing itself—its life to get through. I think… I feel that if it fails, it's going to die," I said. "Or at least significantly injure itself."

"Good."

"Maybe," I said softly, dropping my hand.

Alexa stepped forward, putting her face inches from mine when I attempted to turn away. "What do you mean, maybe?"

"Just that," I said.

"You don't trust."

"I trust. Well, you," I said, pointing at her. "You're a good person. Even if you try to act like you're not, you're a good person. You went with me to find Corey. You let him off the hook for abandoning us. You're there with me for all of my quests, no matter what they are.

"But your people? The Templars? They're the same ones who taught you all supernaturals are evil. That the best you can do is have a business relationship with them, be polite and friendly. That in the end, we're all ravening monsters waiting for the worst to come."

"Not you—"

I held my hand up. "I'm a mage. I'm barely better than the monsters you label. At least, by your standards," I said.

"That's…" Alexa's lips tightened as she shut her mouth, unable to refute it. I could see the war on her face, the struggle between the deeply rooted beliefs in mercy and charity of her original faith fighting against the indoctrination of the Templars and their own experiences. I watched as conflict flickered across her face before she exhaled, pushing the discussion aside. "What do you intend to do?"

I paused, uncertain. In the end, I had to either blindly trust a group that had already shown itself to be somewhat untrustworthy and fanatical in their beliefs, or I could release something dangerous into the world. On that side of the equation, I had the assurance from Caleb saying whatever I released wasn't "that" dangerous, but I also knew Caleb was looking at it from the perspective of a master mage, one who saw threats in city-wide scales.

The monster I might release might only be good enough to kill a city block, but that would be little consolation to the victims. Could I, would I potentially condemn others to death? Where, in all this, did I stand? What right did I have to make these decisions?

"Is the mage done yet? Some of us have better things to do," a voice said, breaking into my thoughts, shrill and high and pitched to ensure I'd heard. My lips twisted, and I realized we'd been standing there for ages, my body wracked with indecision. Damn it.

"Let's do this," I said, gesturing for Alexa to follow me. Whatever thoughts I had, whatever doubts, I had come this far. Perhaps sealing the creature within, effectively killing it, was the wrong choice, but right now, I just did not have enough information to contradict the Templars. And for all the distasteful beliefs they had, they had spent centuries protecting humanity. Perhaps a touch of trust was reasonable.

***

"I'm starting," I called out, my hand on the iron chain while the other slowly worked the various materials into the damaged walls. Most of this prep work had been done already, the materials installed and reworked. Now, under the influence of the spell I was casting, the materials melted and shifted, adjusting themselves and accepting the ritual formulas I was installing in them.

Step by step, spell formulas hovering in my mind, Alexa next to me with my notebook for reminders when I needed them, we walked the perimeter of the building. Of course, it wasn't that simple. The building itself was broken up by hallways and rooms, forcing me to traverse around obstructions. It was at these times I'd scurry forward as the burden of keeping the ritual empowered fell upon the nuns directly.

Step by step, the ritual was patched, but as each section that had been damaged was fixed, the amount of power flowing through the ritual circle increased. The requirements for keeping the channel open jumped as our strength weakened.

"How many more?" Alexa asked as we hurried out of the boiler room.

"Two," I said shortly, saving my breath for more important things, like oxygenating my blood.

"Goo—" Alexa jerked to a halt when the entire building trembled. Eyes wide, we both stared around us as dust floated in the air, and the building slowly settled. "Earthquake?"

"Suuure?" I said uncertainly. The building moved, but it had felt wrong somehow. Before I had time to pin down exactly what the problem was, the entire building shuddered again. And then I realized, the building moved but not the floor. "What's going on?"

My answer came a moment later as a wave of corrupted mana rolled over us. I stretched my senses out, reaching toward the room, and sensed it then, the way the inner ritual circle was fracturing, the way the ritual's weaknesses were widening. I tensed, waiting as I stood there, my hand outstretched and my senses extended to the maximum.

Smash

I felt it when the impact happened that time, felt the changes in the ritual circle, the way the ritual then shifted the impact into the building itself to blunt some of the force. I felt how the ritual's cracks widened and the gush of mana as the impact faded.

"It's attacking the inner circle," I said, my eyes wide.

"It?"

"Whatever is trapped in there," I said, biting my lip. My mind spun as I searched for options and considered the ritual. I had no true understanding of the inner circle. I just did not have the ability to patch it together. Any attempt would be more likely to cause problems than solve them.

"Get the children out!" Alexa snapped to one of the few free staff members. They nodded and scurried upstairs while Alexa tried to reassure the trapped staff we would have things fixed. Of course, the way she kept throwing glances at me while she was speaking informed me she might be less certain of that than she said.

Fix the secondary ritual? That made the most sense theoretically. If we fixed it, the reinforced inner ritual might gain sufficient power to stop whatever it was from coming out. Certainly, it'd stabilize somewhat, but with the inner circle even more damaged than previously, could it hold up? Or would I be pouring power into a faulty line?

"Henry!" Alexa snapped at me as I dithered once again, attempting to divine the best solution. Unlike my gaming sessions, I had no time. No time to hesitate, no time to consider all the best options and come up with something smart and cool. I just had to decide.

I crouched, grabbing the chain from the ground and flooded my mana within, taking hold of the spell that had been supported by others. I kept my mana flowing, taking the burden off the staff while I spoke.

"Everybody leaves."

"What? No. This—"

"I can't stop the inner circle from crumbling. If we pour more power into it, I can't guarantee it won't explode. With the amount of mana that's been stored inside the circle and the compound, the chain reaction could be explosive," I said, explaining quickly even as I reached for the spell formulas I had left open. I quickly tied them off as I ran other calculations. "The staff can go. I'll shut down the ritual, maybe even… Yes, invert the ritual, pull the mana out, and disperse.

"Have them tear up the ritual at the fence when they're out. Get the kids out. I'll keep the inner ritual contained for four—no, five minutes."

"We can help you hold it up!" one of the nuns barked, but I noticed a few others had already left the chain, rushing onward to inform others.

I shook my head in negation and pointed upward. "Kids."

I saw the conflict on their faces, the struggle. Their duty to the children won out over their stubbornness and distrust. With a nod, they let go and headed up the stairs, the commotion from above slowly increasing in volume. The pounding of feet, the raised voices of children and teenagers who tumbled around in surprise, it all filtered from above and reinforced my conviction to keep this ramshackle, hodgepodge of magic holding.

Desires were weak shields against the spears of reality. With the nuns gone, I was bearing the cost of keeping multiple rituals open. Even as I shut the open connections down, finishing the patches one by one, I was also opening other areas, inverting certain aspects of the runes. The burden kept increasing, making me grit my teeth as energy continued to course out of me.

Then, blessed relief. As if someone had joined me in pushing a car, I felt mana flowing again in the chain. This mana was cleaner, brighter than the others. Not pure but lighter and hopeful. There was only one person who I knew who passed that kind of mana on.

"Alexa?"

"Don't bother asking. It's my job, remember?" Alexa said softly. Refocusing on the real world, I saw her stationed facing down the corridor, one hand on the chain, the other holding her spear, glowing with a pure, bright light.

"Thanks."
"Just do your thing," Alexa said.
And to that, I could only nod.

Chapter 18

Carry the two, multiple by eight hundred and fifty-three, integral of the result… Use Roland's Fourth Law of Motion on the result, add Kaylee's Sub-planar Integration Formula but swap the third and eighth lines out. My mind swam with formulas and calculations that were one part math, one part mystic formulas, and the last part intuition. Apply vigorously to close the open ritual circle.

Next.

My left hand clenched around the chain, feeding mana into the ritual circle. My right twisted and jerked as I used a physical component to substitute for portions of the formula while I chanted aloud. Pressure continued to increase, mana dropped, and still, there were four more open connections and three areas I needed to invert.

Worst of all, we could only continue to feed the power in until I flicked the switch on the ritual. That meant the creature within the inner circle continued to bash at it without cease, not knowing we were going to release it anyway. It meant each attack sent a jarring force through the building, adding cracks that spread and knocked dust around. In addition, the blowback from the impacts toward the second ritual circle was painful to say the least and always took a few precious seconds to recover from.

Overall, even with all that, we were nearly done when the abbess finally made her way back to us. The elderly matron frowned at the pair of us, the way Alexa glowed and I was twitching and jerking as power flooded through my body.

"Will the ritual hold?" the abbess asked.

"It won't," Alexa replied. "Henry is inverting the ritual to disperse the mana. Is the circle at the fence broken?"

"It is," the abbess said with a frown. "How did this happen? You assured me the ritual would hold until it was fixed."

"I didn't expect it to be attacked," I said with a snarl while I forced my cramping fingers to continue drawing runes in the air. "I can't make accurate estimates without full information. As *I told you.*"

"There is no reason to shout," the abbess said with a sniff. "And you cannot release the creature."

"What creature?" I snarled. "Don't you think it's about time to tell me?"

"No."

I growled but ignored the woman otherwise. Damn her and her idiotic rules. It didn't matter—not really, since the ritual was coming down, whether she liked it or not.

"Are you still going to release it?" the abbess asked again as I tied off the last open connection. I relaxed slightly when the burden on mana dropped, but only slightly. I still had those points of inversion to complete, and while theoretically it was simple enough to do, that was in theory. If I altered the formula wrong, we'd be looking at, best case, an uncontrolled release of built-up mana. Worst case? Probably an explosion.

Why the hell does the answer for so many things involving magic end with an explosion?

"I'm speaking with you!"

"Busy."

"We are, Sister," Alexa said, cutting in quickly before the abbess could speak again. "It's the safest choice of action. Unless you can give us a very good reason not to."

The abbess fell silent for a moment, giving me time to finish inverting the last section. Now, I just had to verify the actual spell worked before I inserted the inversions. I ran through the ritual circle and the formulas as fast as I could, only barely hearing the abbess speak.

"It's a spirit trapped within. A dark, savage spirit that was too powerful for our people to end when they fought. They managed to weaken it sufficiently to trap it within the initial ritual. After which, our men purchased the building and reinforced the original ritual with the building as you've seen," she said. "We cannot release it. The damage that will occur—"

"Too late," I said softly. "If you'd let us know beforehand, if I'd known… Maybe. But there's too many gaps in the ritual now, too much wear and tear. Even if I wanted to reinforce it, it'd probably tear under the stress."

The abbess's lips thinned and then she nodded as she stepped away from us. She clutched a large cross in front of her body, staring forward at the corridor while I inserted the formulas. At first, nothing happened, but the mana finally kicked in, the switch of the runes occurred, and while the ritual circle glowed and strained, it held.

Held and started siphoning the power from the inner circle, pulling built-up mana into the external circle where it dispersed into the air. With the ritual now powered in another format, I released the chain and the spell, the sudden release of weight making me stagger.

"Alexa…" I croaked out, waving at the chain. I could have saved my voice, since the initiate had released the chain a second after I had. Together we watched the corridor, feeling the building shake again when the creature attempted to free itself.

"How long?" the abbess asked.

"Ten minutes. Maybe less," I said and slumped to the floor with my back against the wall. Damn, my mana well was drained. Feeling within, I could tell I had barely a quarter left, and that was only because I had been doing my best to husband the mana drain. I had a feeling Alexa was not much better, though the initiate refused to sit, her spear pointed at the doorway.

"Can I do anything?" the abbess said.

"A drink would be nice," I said, then laughed softly. "Then just keep everyone back. I'll try to… bargain with it. Or something."

My last waffly sentence received a look of incredulity from the abbess and Alexa, but in truth, it was the best I could do. If the spirit came out willing to talk, perhaps we could. If not, well, I had my spells. And my wards…

Oh. Right. I had my portable wards.

With a groan, I pushed myself up and retrieved my backpack with its blocks of wood and metal. As I moved, I ignored the questioning looks sent my way by both women. Focus. I had to figure out the best way to set these up. Just in case.

***

The silence over the last couple of minutes finally got to Alexa who burst, asking, "What is going on?"

"Waiting," I said. My terse reply got me a glare, which I had to chuckle at. "The spirit's waiting for the ritual to fail completely."

"It can do that?"

"Be a poor spirit that can't sense Mana," I said.

"When?"

"Any time now." As I finished my sentence, a pop like an over-inflated balloon resounded through my soul. Corrupted mana gushed out from the room, the cold, almost slimy darkness of mana, making me shiver again. Eyes narrowed, I pushed myself to my feet. For long seconds, nothing happened, the door still remaining shut. Then with a shudder, the door collapsed outward, and a single, black snout followed by a black paw appeared.

Mentally braced for a creature from the dark, a monster of Lovecraftian proportions, a spirit of the night that sucked souls and flayed humans, I realized what exited the ritual room was so much worse.

"A *skunk spirit*!" I shouted in surprise, my eyes wide. "You trapped a *skunk* spirit?"

"Yes, a creature of darkness."

Skunk Spirit (Level 180) (Weakened Significantly. Current Level 31)
HP: 380/380

"It's a skunk!" I snapped. That explained the corruption in the mana, the way it stopped being "normal." Trapped for decades, the buildup from its scent glands, whether it was intentional or not, would have corrupted the mana around it. Since it was a spirit, its "spray" was of course mana based.

"And they are known to be monsters, even among the natives," the abbess repeated, hand clutching her cross tightly.

"Only in some cultures," I snapped. With our foe turning out to be an angry animal spirit, I was a lot less inclined to hit first and ask questions later.

Stepping forward, I glared at Alexa who moved to block my way until she relented.

Having exited the room, the skunk spirit had shrunk its body slightly to better handle the small space it now occupied. It was now only the size of a large dog, the kind that fought off wolf packs before lolling in front of a fireplace, its shepherd owner seated beside it. The spirit's time trapped away with limited access to new mana had damaged the creature. Its fur was ratty, tattered and spotty in places, while its head was slightly misshapen and bleeding from a bone-deep opening. I assumed the last was from its repeated attacks against the ward.

"Brother Skunk," I said slowly, stopping a good distance away and well behind the line of my Shield Wards. I wanted—I needed to give the spirit a chance, but that didn't mean I was going to put my neck on the chopping block. "We mean you no harm."

The spirit did not speak at first, though hearing my voice made it stare directly at me. I gulped slightly, the spirit's hostility bathing my battered senses before it began to amble forward.

"Brother Skunk, I need to know your intentions before I let you go farther. Can you speak?" I said, trying again.

"It's useless. It's a dumb spirit," the abbess growled. "Kill it while it's weak, before it hurts anyone!"

"*You will die first, cross wielder.*" The spirit's voice appeared in our minds with a hiss and raging fury. But as surprising as it was that it could speak to us directly, I noted there seemed a thread of weakness in its voice, one deeply hidden but there still.

"You speak, Brother Skunk. That's great," I said, forcing a smile on my face.

"*You are no brother of mine, false shaman,*" the skunk said, "*but your actions have been mildly favorable. Leave now, and we will part without enmity.*"

"About that. You wouldn't mind telling me what you intend, do you? Just that, I'm pretty sure my friend isn't about to leave," I said, glancing at where Alexa stood silently, spear leveled at the spirit.

"*I seek revenge. For being trapped. I shall tear their bones from their flesh and feast on their bodies to regain my strength.*"

"See. What did I tell you!" the abbess shrieked. From behind her back, she pulled a vial of holy water.

"That's, umm, a bit extreme."

"*They trapped me for decades!*"

"Yeah, I get that. Their bad," I said, grimacing. The spirit was right. It had been trapped. Of course, the Templars might have had a good reason for doing so, like the creature having killed and eaten others, but I had no context for its initial imprisonment. And while I was leaning toward a knockdown, drag-out fight, I was still leery of it. Weakened as it might be, it was a nature spirit, a powerful one at that. For all intents and purposes, I was an apprentice mage with low mana and dodgy defense. If I could talk it out, I would. "I'm sure there's a middle ground. I mean, you don't go around killing everyone who annoys you, right?"

Truth be told, I was betting a lot on some half-remembered Native American stories. Not all tribes considered skunks evil, though a few did. They could also be considered protectors, guardians, and pacifist creatures. If the stories were to hold true to some extent, then the spirit before me was no more dangerous than any other wild animal.

"You ask me to negotiate, to barter. When the perpetrators of my imprisonment stand beside you." The skunk spirit twisted its head side to side, its tail swaying dangerously as it sat up high. Even from here, I could feel how the mana around me grew more and more corrupted as the mana from the room mixed with it. Casting spells in this environment was going to be incredibly difficult.

"Yeah…" I said, hesitating visibly and looking at the abbess. "You should leave."

"I will not! This is my building."

"Just go. If it gets down to a fight, you can always beat on it when it comes up the stairs." I locked gazes with the abbess. I could feel the pressure of her gaze, the resolute will behind it, but I had my stubbornness and right behind me. And a lot of adrenaline. Eventually, she broke her gaze and turned away, hurrying up the stairs but not before issuing one final warning to be careful.

I turned toward Alexa who had been watching the quietly recuperating spirit. She just looked at me, and I knew better than to request her to leave.

"That do?" I asked the spirit.

"*You still stand with the other.*"

"She wasn't even born when you were put in there. Alexa has done nothing to you, nor has she even offended you. She's just here for my protection," I said.

"*And what makes you so special, false shaman?*" the spirit asked, curiosity aroused. It padded forward, sniffing the air as it neared the ward line. I gritted my teeth, getting ready to throw it up if the creature charged. But as if it knew what the ward blocks were for, it stopped and paced next to the blocks, eyeing me first from one side, then to the next. "*I smell another spirit on you. And on her. An old one. A foreign one.*"

"Lily," I said slowly. "Look. You're free. We can work out a… a compromise and restitution for your imprisonment if you promise not to kill any humans or other, well, civilized beings." When the spirit began to bristle and aim its tail, I added hurriedly, saying, "Other than in self-defense."

"*Do you think I am that cruel, human?*"

"No. Just have to be sure, you know?" I said slowly. There were certainly some things I just wasn't supposed to tell the truth on. "So, can we deal?"

"*Perhaps. But I fear you have little to offer me.*"

I exhaled loudly when I realized we were getting somewhere. A "perhaps" meant it was thinking, and if it was thinking of it, we could talk. I grinned widely, opening my hands wide as I got ready to bargain. Right. What did skunks eat anyway?

***

"I don't believe it worked," Alexa said, awe in her voice when the nuns came trotting down with another pile of nuts, berries, and eggs. All organic of course. In fact, the children had been assigned the task of washing all the produce with distilled water just in case.

"Ixnay on the worksay!" I whispered to the initiate.

"Pretty sure that's not how pig Latin works," Alexa replied softly, "but he's eating, right?"

"Yes, but he only promised not to cause harm for the next day," I said and eyed the fur of the creature slowly unclumping and gaining a healthy glow.

"Well, yes, but…" Alexa paused, then looked at me more seriously. "Do you think he'll break his word?"

"No, but Murphy is always listening." To this, Alexa could only nod.

In wary silence, we watched as the spirit gorged itself on produce, but eventually, the first delivery was complete. What used to be a bedraggled, scruffy spirit was replaced by a sleek animal, one whose fur had been combed and unmatted. The wound itself had stopped bleeding, having crusted over, and the patches in its fur had begun growing out. Still, it was clear the spirit had only recovered mildly and was not fully healed.

"So, Spirit Skunk…" I said slowly, letting my voice trail off as it finished preening itself.

"*You have completed your side of the bargain. I shall not eat the cross bearers so long as they continue to fulfill their side of the bargain. Once a week, they will provide gifts of this form,*" the skunk said.

"They can do that. Right?" I said the last word to the abbess who stiffly nodded, unhappiness on her face. I sighed, relaxing slightly when she did nod. As the agreement was completed, the various members of the orphanage started evacuating, opening a clear passage for the spirit to leave. While they did that and the skunk checked the bowls for anything that remained, I eyed the building and the cracks that now covered the walls. "That's not good."

"No. I've probably failed the quest," Alexa said, her face perfectly serene.

"Wait… what?" I exclaimed in surprise. And then my brain finally caught up with me. Right. The goal was to keep the orphanage open. There was no way the building inspectors were going to miss the damage or allow the orphanage to last. I eyed the spirit evilly for a brief moment before discarding the idea of making it help with the repairs. Among other things, I wasn't sure I'd trust a nature spirit to fix man-made buildings. The ensuing results were likely to be less than optimal. "Can the contractors help?"

"Not in time," Alexa said with a grimace. "The inspections were to happen this Monday. Even if they worked all weekend…"

"It wouldn't be enough," I said with a huff. Right. Could I—

"*I shall leave now, false shaman*" the skunk said, punching its words into my mind. I winced, repatching my mental defenses while offering the creature a nod in agreement. Right. Lead the spirit out. I gestured down the corridor and then walked ahead while Alexa squirrelled herself in a side corridor to act as rear guard. Or, you know, stab it in the back if it tried something.

With all the staff members and kids out of the building—or out of sight at least—the three of us made our way toward the exit. There was an almost farcical moment when the spirit got stuck on the narrow stairways, squirming its body around the narrow walls and damaging them further with its rather long, sharp claws. By the time it exited the stairwell, the orphanage had another portion to fix.

When it exited, the skunk splayed its claws slightly and tilted its head side to side as it sniffed the air and its tail rose behind it. I frowned and watched the damn spirit, wondering what had it riled up now.

"You humans have destroyed the world even more. Even the stink of your people has grown," it said with a snarl.

"Eh…" I stared at the skunk spirit, struck by the absurdity of it calling anything odorous. Then again… "Our deal is still true, right?" I asked, my voice low and slow.

"Yes." The skunk snorted and took a few more steps forward. It stopped suddenly, its tail flaring again, and turned its head to face an empty spot in the garden. "I smell you!"

There was no movement at first, but suddenly a light ripple occurred. Standing in the spot where the skunk was watching, three men clad in light chainmail carrying swords and shields appeared. Thankfully, they weren't using guns. Among other things, while it was easy to enchant a gun, enchanting bullets were another matter, and since they weren't fighting a physical creature using normal bullets, even those lined with something like silver would be of little use. Even rock salt, a popular weapon against ghosts, was of little use here.

Spirits were only affected by two things reliably: magic and magically enchanted weapons. Even cold iron was a hit-or-miss subject depending on the spirit in question. Thus, it was no surprise to me the weapons and armor the Templars were wearing glowed with the light of enchantment in my eyes. What was a surprise was their presence.

Knight Templar (Level 84)
HP: 180/180

"*Betrayal!*" the skunk snarled at me, its feet shifting to pull its body away. Alexa, in the meantime, moved from behind it toward my body, crouching low with her spear held up in guard position.

"Wait! No. I didn't have anything to do with this. And, you guys! Stand the hell down," I said, noting how the Templars had moved closer when the skunk had shifted.

The lead Templar spoke up, his eyes hard and dismissive. "Initiate Dubough. You have failed your assessment. Spectacularly. It remains to be seen if you will even continue to be allowed to wear the cross."

Alexa stiffened at his words, a slight tremble appearing in her hands.

"Hey!" I said. "There's no reason to speak with Alexa that way. We did the best we could, considering you morons refused to give us further information. This could have been avoided if you'd actually been more forthcoming." When I realized what I'd said, where I said it, I turned toward the spirit and waved a hand weakly. "Though, it's good that you're free. Because you're not going to hurt anyone. Right?"

"I was wrong. You are too foolish to betray me. But if they attack, I will eat them."

I straightened slightly, trying to decide if I was more insulted or relieved by the spirit's announcement. What it didn't do was stop the Templars from continuing to close in.

With a huff, I raised my hand and focused. A Force Shield was basically a projection of power to an area that stopped further motion. One thing I had realized was that Lily's spell was slightly different from the more common shield spells used by modern mages. Most of those "froze" air directly, stilling the molecules and creating a wall to block attacks or, in other cases, used other physical elements to block attacks. The Force Shield Lily had provided me actually worked by stilling motion in the area of effect. From the outside, it looked the same, though it did offer me a few applications others might not have available.

In this case, it mattered not one whit. The Force Shield I created was basically a wall, set to appear and extend a good nine feet in the air. The size of the wall was a bit problematic, requiring a significant amount of mana, but it did halt the Templars' advances. With a bump.

"Are you acting against us, mage?" The lead Templar's hand clenched around his sword as he eyed the wall, a vein along his temple visibly throbbing and highlighting his pale-blond hair. The skunk spirit on the other hand was watching the entire thing, rather than fleeing.

"Just keeping my word," I said.

"Initiate Dubough!" the blond Templar snarled.

"Henry…" Alexa said hesitantly as she looked back at me. I saw her hand tremble as the point of her spear wavered between me and the skunk.

"What are you going to do, Alexa? Stab me?" I asked, lips pursed. I didn't put up a shield, didn't step away. It wouldn't help. I didn't have enough mana to keep two shields going, not after all this. The best I could hope for was to stop the Templars from reaching the spirit briefly while it ran away. Which reminded me… "Hey, Skunky. Time to go. If you don't, ain't my fault."

"*Skunky?*" the spirit snarled, its tail flaring higher.

I winced slightly, but I had little attention to spare for the spirit. Right now, I had a much more serious threat in front of me, one whose hesitation was visible on her face.

"Initiate. Why are you hesitating? Knock out the mage and allow us to finish this vile creature."

"It's not though," Alexa whispered softly in defiance. "It's not." Her voice grew louder. "It just wants to live. We were the ones who trapped it first. Forced it—"

"It is a pagan creature," the Templar said, his voice growing strident. "One that is likely to cause harm if left unchecked."

"And so we trap it? Kill it?" Alexa asked, her eyes tight. "It might not believe in our Lord, but it is still a creature He made, and so long as it harms no one, should we not allow it the chance to come to the Lord on its own free will?"

"It is not human," the Templar said. "It was not made in His image."

"It still lives and thinks. It can still choose." Alexa looked at the creature. "And who are we to judge him? Is that not reserved for our Lord? Especially for actions it has yet to take."

"Initiate… no. No longer an initiate," the Templar said. "I hereby declare, with the power vested in me as the Knight Templar superintendent of the third division, that Alexa Dumough, formerly an initiate of the Knights Templar, is from now on no longer a part of our order. Henceforth, any and all action taken by Alexa Dumough will have no association with the Knights Templar."

The words were like a blow to Alexa, each sentence causing her to jerk. When he finished, Alexa straightened and turned toward them, her spear aimed at the trio without hesitation or trembling. Though, as she turned away, I noted how red her eyes were and the light glint of tears on her cheeks.

"Morons," I mumbled. I'd add more, but before I could, the Templar gestured, and his buddies hammered the wall with their swords. The enchanted blades sent tangible feedback through my spell, making my knees buckle for a second before I forced them straight.

"Child!" the Templar snarled, but I noted how he did not move to attempt to harm me. Obviously they had read Alexa's reports. There was no way Lily would allow them to harm me. Well, unless she considered this a social challenge, at which point I might take a bit of damage, but they didn't need to know that.

"Oh, yeah. I'm the one with the monovision of how the world should work," I snapped. Child indeed. These guys were like five-year-olds who were so definite in their view of the world, nothing—not even logic—could sway their mind.

Another blow and the Force Shield began to crumble. Finally the skunk spirit decided it had had enough and turned tail, bounding toward the fence. This made the Templars speed up their attacks on my Shield Wall. After the second consecutive set of blows, I could no longer hold the wall and it shattered. As the skunk crouched near the fence, its lips peeled apart at the charging Templars and raised its tail. This time around, I had a feeling it wasn't just threatening.

"MOVE!" I shouted at Alexa, grabbing for her arm. I missed because the initiate—sorry, ex-initiate—had moved faster than me, having spun around, and reached for my own shoulder as she took off running for the door. I stumbled and followed along as fast as I could.

We almost made it.

The explosive spray covered ground fast, swamping the Templars first. They, unlike us, were ready for the assault, however, each of them clutching a cross around their waist that glowed with mana. The radiance from the cross covered their body, pushing against the spray and its noxious vapors. A part of me wondered how that spell managed to separate air from the spray itself—if it did. The rest of me was gagging, the vanguard of the spray reaching us already.

The door was thrust open by Alexa, and I was hauled in before it slammed shut. Not before the first wave of the spray entered though, causing the pair of us to bowl over, retching from the smell as our eyes watered and our skin prickled. Together, we staggered away from the door which was slowly allowing even more of the pervasive smell in.

"Henry…" Alexa croaked helplessly as we stumbled deeper into the abandoned orphanage. I understood her point. This smell from the spirit was more than just offensive; it was directly affecting the mana uptake and disbursement that occurred naturally. It had, basically, corrupted the mana all around, the direct effect of its earlier mana corruption multiplied a hundred times.

"The gym." I hacked and coughed as I dragged Alexa to the room. Together, we burst through the double doors and felt relief almost immediately—at least from the mana effects, though the spray that stayed on our skin continued to irritate our bodies.

"First-aid kit…" Alexa said as she stood, stumbling away. I ran my mana in a simple Heal spell, pushing the edges of the irritation away, but as I sat up, I could not help but consider how bad things were, out there.

"We can't stay here," I announced even as I fumbled my bag off my shoulder. After pulling a block out, I began the frantic process of empowering it. Thankfully, the work around the fences and the gym had provided the blueprint for the enchantment I was casting.

Empower Cast
Synchronization Rate: 82%

Cleanse Cast
Synchronization Rate: 72%

Yes! I tossed the block out, directly through the open doorway and watched as it landed in the hallway. The pair of linked spells began to work immediately, slowly grinding away at the corrupted mana. I watched for a moment to ensure the spell worked, watched the fluctuations in the spell formulas and then nodded.

Right. If I adjusted the third and eleventh line with Gaspard's Second Elemental Rune, it should stabilize and increase the speed of the mana cleansing. Lips parted, I began the process of empowering the next wooden block.

As I tossed the second block away and reached for another, I was stopped by a hand on mine. I frowned, my eyes bloodshot and my nose clogged and snotty as I stared at the blonde faith healer who had a rag and pail in hand.

"What?" I said.

"Stop. You're already low on mana. Take a few minutes, let me clean you up," Alexa said, holding the rag up. Rather than protest, I sat quietly as she quickly worked me over, swabbing me with the sharp-smelling, slightly soapy rag.

"What is that?"

"Hydrogen peroxide, dishwashing liquid, and baking soda," Alexa said. "I had to run out to the kitchen to get the last two, but luckily the kitchen is well insulated."

"How…"

"Faith healer, remember? My ability let me push the miasma away. Now, hold still."

When I tried to take the rag away, Alexa glared at me and I gave up. Rather than fight her on this, instead I focused on the next step. Two empowered cleansing blocks should be enough for the building, eventually. Of course, more would be better, but at least the doorway itself was fixed. The concern was the miasma that had spread—was spreading—throughout the neighborhood. It needed stopping.

Which meant…

Pendants. Or at least something to increase our resistance again and shield us against the miasma. I drew a ragged breath, testing my mana limits once again. The time resting while watching the skunk eat had allowed me to regenerate most of my mana, but it had taken a beating when the Templars had done their drum act on my channeled Force Shield.

If we could contain more of the miasma, the blocks I had contained and the runes around the gym would eventually deal with the mana taint, but—

"You're frowning harder than Father did when we brought back the *Evil Dead II* movie," Alexa said, prodding me sharply. "What is it?"

"That's…" I shook my head and pushed it aside. No. Not right now. "I don't have the mana. We need to fix the fence, but I don't have the mana to fix the pendants and the fence."

"Then don't," Alexa said, offering me a hand up. "I can shield us both."

"Can you?"

"Yes. I might not be an initiate, but my faith has not changed. Nor our Father's favor," Alexa said confidently.

I drew a deep breath but nodded, grabbing my trusty backpack. "Then, let's do this."

We didn't have time to wait.

Chapter 19

Outside, almost immediately, we were assaulted by the miasma. It attempted to cling to our bodies, to our skin, but the low, brilliant glow of power covering us pushed the miasma back and kept it from sticking. On the way, I scooped up the pair of blocks and dropped one off as we exited the building.

Outside, the effects of the miasma were already telling. The grass had taken on a slightly greyish tinge, the leaves on the tree curling up slightly. All around, I heard the hacking and coughing of individuals caught in the cloud, their bodies weakening as the mana they unconsciously circulated was slowly corrupted further and further.

Together, we hurried toward the fence. I found myself turning my head constantly as I attempted to locate both the Templars and the spirit. I noted neither were present, which was for the better at least. Hopefully, the skunk spirit had managed to get away. Otherwise, all of this had been for nothing. Then again, considering the amount of damage it had caused by its defensive measure, perhaps the Templars were right. Of course, that would be a better sell if the Templars hadn't triggered the entire incident by being obstinate asses, so the entire incident could be considered as wash.

At the fence itself, we quickly found the first break in the runes. I frowned at the hastily scratched out rune and grunted. Fixing it with Mend—the physical portion anyway—was possible. It would just require delicately adjusting the spell formula while it worked, a slight alteration from my usual, almost careless use of the spell.

Mend Cast
Synchronicity 64%

Minutes later, I finally had the rune fixed. When I opened my eyes, the rune was indeed fixed if slightly worse off than before. With my practiced eye, I could see where the rune had not been mended correctly, where the lines were off, but as they said, it was good enough for office work.

"Next," I said out loud.

We moved, shifting from spot to spot on the fence until we found another broken rune. Thankfully, there weren't many, and they were mostly clustered close together. Each of them required Mend, but luckily that was not a mana-intensive spell, especially since the fixing I was doing was relatively minute. Still, toward the end, my head was throbbing again.

"How much longer?" Alexa asked, pushing against my arm slightly to get my attention.

"Just have to restart the spell," I said softly, wincing as my head throbbed. When Alexa opened her mouth to ask, I just shook my head. Instead, I suited action to my words and raised my free hand and pressed it against the runes.

Restart the spell. It was easy, since most of the runes were already enchanted. I just needed to feed enough mana into the rune structure, fill the empty spots with the actual correct spell formulas, and *blammo*. Containment ritual complete.

Simple. If I wasn't already running on fumes. If my head didn't throb like a jackhammer. If the mana around me wasn't corrupted and impossible to refresh myself from. Simple. I shuddered as mana flowed from me, drawn forth and pushed ahead by my will. My head throbbed further, my vision greying out as the light that encompassed us dimmed slightly, Alexa struggling to protect us. Simple. I licked my lips, a slight warmth and iron taste appearing on my tongue as the liquid flowed away. I reached out with my other hand unconsciously, wiping at the nose bleed even as the spell formulas danced in my mind and runes slid into place.

Simple.

With a thrum, the ritual burst into being around us. The press of mana on the ritual, a spell so intimately connected to me, made me waver. I frowned, noting how the world was leaning backward slightly and realized I was losing my balance. With a sweep of her feet, Alexa dropped me into her waiting arms and the princess carried me back into the orphanage.

"Block," I managed to cough out, waving despairingly at my bag.

After a moment, Alexa pulled the second block out and tossed it onto the grounds before dragging my limp body into the gym. Inside, she sagged to the floor, sweat matting her pale hair.

"Lily's going to kill us," she said with a groan, obviously imagining how the jinn was going to complain about my mana overdraw. I wished I could answer her, but lying on the comfortable floor, my eyes decided it was time to close.

***

When I next woke, it was to the insistent prodding from Alexa hours later. With the major concentration captured within the fence, the remaining escaped mana had slowly dispersed or been cleansed. That left the pair of overworked empowered blocks to finish up the job on the inside. Unfortunately, I had also left the orphanage staff with pendants, which is how the abbess had managed to make her way back to glare at us.

"I know, I know. Leave," I said with a huff.

"You and Ms. Dumough are no longer welcome," the abbess pronounced, and I sighed. Well, duh.

"Of course." Alexa bobbed her head in acknowledgement. "And I apologize again about the damage… and failing the orphanage."

"Yes, you should be." The abbess paused, then continued, her voice softer and slightly kinder. "However, the Templars have informed us that they have ensured we will be given the requisite time to complete the projects. And made a sizeable donation to deal with the inconveniences we have faced."

I paused, my eyes wide. "Wait. They could have fixed this? Then why didn't they?"

"This was a test," the abbess said, her voice calm.

"But—"

"Henry." Alexa placed a hand on my arm and shook her head.

"Why aren't you angry about this!" I said, waving a hand around. "This, this was garbage. We went through all this for nothing!"

"Garbage?" Alexa asked softly, then shook her head. "We freed a spirit that was imprisoned for decades. We helped slow the spread of a dangerous drug. And... Okay, the mushrooms weren't particularly useful."

I snorted.

"But I also learned something about myself. And them."

"What? Self-knowledge is the best knowledge?" I asked sarcastically. Sure, the test itself probably never placed the kids in any real danger, now that I knew what had been kept below. The skunk spirit might have been angry, and we might have ended up fighting it, but the abbess would never have let the children be around during such a battle. Even the mana poisoning had been a slow process, one that could easily have been fixed with a trip outdoors, but still—

"Yes," Alexa said serenely.

I glared at the ex-initiate, but in the last six hours, she seemed to have gained a sense of peace over her decision. I opened my mouth to prod her further before I shut it. There had been flash in her eyes when I was about to speak. Perhaps she might have accepted her decision and the consequences, but the pain was still there. In the end, it wasn't my place to prod her.

"Fine," I grumped and then looked at the abbess who just stared at us serenely. I sighed and waved a hand goodbye at the woman, tromping outward. "Let's go, partner."

"Coming." Even without looking around, I could hear the smile in her voice.

Epilogue

Of course it wasn't that easy. Once we got back, I had to explain the new situation to my other watcher. Caleb was less than impressed with my various explanations and the fact that I overdrew my mana, again. In fact, after some testing, he relegated me to a two-month period of convalescence and book study. It seemed my constant abuse of my body had damaged my mana channels.

As for Caleb's thoughts on Alexa? The mage did not deign to inform me.

Alexa, on the other hand, had a more arduous time of it. She had a number of belongings still at the camp which had been returned to us. In turn, Alexa returned a number of smaller items I had never noticed her owning till then, including a surprising number of explosives. Interestingly enough, the Templars allowed her to keep her spear and armor. As a mostly secret organization, none of her materials had designs on them, so they did not require cleansing.

Perhaps the greatest shock of all for the ex-initiate was the closure of her bank account and the return of a small portion of funds within it. Once I was back on my feet, I helped Alexa run a number of "adult" errands including opening a bank account and applying for a credit card. As a former ward of the Templars, she had never needed to do either herself.

Without the salary and funds provided by the Templars, Alexa quickly began running the various quests on the board that she could handle while I convalesced. If I didn't know better, I would have said she was distracting herself from the abrupt change in her. But I did, and late-night sobs from her room indicated that, newfound serenity or not, Alexa still had much to work through.

As for myself? The longer I existed in this strange new world, the more I realized how simplistic my earlier perceptions on it had been. There were deep currents, not only among the organizations that existed here but within those currents. A single misstep could pull me under. As it stood, I knew the Templars were waiting. And now, I could not help but wonder, who else?

The End

Author's Note

Thank you for reading my attempt at an urban fantasy GameLit world. This book was a struggle to write as I wanted to focus on Alexa and the choices she had to make along with Henry's growing understanding and comfort in the supernatural world.

As always, if you enjoyed reading the book, please do leave a review and rating. It makes a big difference in sales. Read on for the conclusion in book 3:

- A Jinn's Wish
  https://books2read.com/jinns-wish

In addition, please check out my other series, the Adventures on Brad (a slice-of-life fantasy LitRPG), the System Apocalypse (a post-apocalyptic LitRPG) and A Thousand Li (a cultivation xanxia series). Book one of each series is named:

- A Healer's Gift (Book 1 of the Adventures on Brad)
  https://books2read.com/healers-gift
- Life in the North (An Apocalyptic LitRPG)
  https://readerlinks.com/l/729295
- A Thousand Li (a cultivation series inspired by Chinese wuxia and xianxia novels)
  https://readerlinks.com/l/729231

For more great information about LitRPG series, check out the Facebook groups:
    - Gamelit Society
https://www.facebook.com/groups/LitRPGsociety/
    - LitRPG Books
https://www.facebook.com/groups/LitRPG.books/

If you'd like to support me directly, I now have a Patreon page where previews of all my new books can be found!

- https://www.patreon.com/taowong

About the Author

Tao Wong is an avid fantasy and sci-fi reader who spends his time working and writing in the North of Canada. He's spent way too many years doing martial arts of many forms, and having broken himself too often, he now spends his time writing about fantasy worlds.

For updates on the series and his other books (and special one-shot stories), please visit the author's website: http://www.mylifemytao.com

Subscribers to Tao's mailing list will receive exclusive access to short stories in the Thousand Li and System Apocalypse universes: https://www.subscribepage.com/taowong

Or visit Tao's Facebook Page: https://www.facebook.com/taowongauthor/

About the Publisher

Starlit Publishing is wholly owned and operated by Tao Wong. It is a science fiction and fantasy publisher focused on the LitRPG & cultivation genres. Their focus is on promoting new, upcoming authors in the genre whose writing challenges the existing stereotypes while giving a rip-roaring good read.

For more information on Starlit Publishing, visit their website: https://www.starlitpublishing.com/

You can also join Starlit Publishing's mailing list to learn of new, exciting authors and book releases. https://starlitpublishing.com/newsletter-signup/

Life in the North – Sample Chapter 1

Greetings citizen. As a peaceful and organised immersion into the Galactic Council has been declined (extensively and painfully we might add), your world has been declared a Dungeon World. Thank you. We were getting bored with the 12 that we had previously.

Please note that the process of developing a Dungeon World can be difficult for current inhabitants. We recommend leaving the planet till the process is completed in 373 days, 2 hours, 14 minutes and 12 seconds.

For those of you unable or unwilling to leave, do note that new Dungeons and wandering monsters will spawn intermittently throughout the integration process. All new Dungeons and zones will receive recommended minimum levels, however, during the transition period expect there to be significant volatility in the levels and types of monsters in each Dungeon and zone.

As a new Dungeon World, your planet has been designated a free-immigration location. Undeveloped worlds in the Galactic Council may take advantage of this new immigration policy. Please try not to greet all new visitors the same way as you did our Emissary, you humans could do with some friends.

As part of the transition, all sentient subjects will have access to new classes and skills as well as the traditional user interface adopted by the Galactic Council in 119 GC.
Thank you for your co-operation and good luck! We look forward to meeting you soon.

Time to System initiation: 59 minutes 23 seconds

I groan, freeing my hand enough to swipe at the blue box in front of my face as I crank my eyes open. Weird dream. It's not as if I had drunk that much either, just a few shots of whiskey before I went to bed. Almost as soon as the box disappears, another appears, obscuring the small 2-person tent that I'm sleeping in.

Congratulations! You have been spawned in the Kluane National Park (Level 110+) zone.
You have received 7,500 XP (Delayed)

As per Dungeon World Development Schedule 124.3.2.1, inhabitants assigned to a region with a recommended Level 25 or more above the inhabitants' current Level will receive one Small perk.

As per Dungeon World Development Schedule 124.3.2.2, inhabitants assigned to a region with a recommended Level 50 or more above the inhabitants' current Level will receive one Medium perk.

As per Dungeon World Development Schedule 124.3.2.3, inhabitants assigned to a region with a recommended Level 75 or more above the inhabitants' current Level will receive one Large perk.

As per Dungeon World Development Schedule 124.3.2.4, inhabitants assigned to a region with a recommended Level 100 or more above the inhabitants' current Level will receive one Greater perk

What the hell? I jerk forwards and almost fall immediately backwards, the sleeping bag tangling me up. I scramble out, pulling my 5' 8" frame into a sitting position as I swipe black hair out of my eyes to stare at the taunting blue message. Alright, I'm awake and this is not a dream.

This can't be happening, I mean, sure it's happening, but it can't be. It must be a dream, things like this didn't happen in real life. However, considering the rather realistic aches and pains that encompass my body from yesterday's hike, it's really not a dream. Still, this can't be happening.

When I reach out, attempting to touch the screen itself and for a moment, nothing happens until I move my hand when the screen seems to 'stick' to it, swinging with my hand. It's almost like a window in a touchscreen which makes no sense, since this is the real world and there's no tablet. Now that I'm concentrating, I can even feel how the screen has a slight tactile sensation to it, like touching plastic wrap stretched too tight except with the added tingle of static electricity. I stare at my hand and the window and then flick it away watching the window shrink. This makes no sense.

Just yesterday I had hiked up the King's Throne Peak with all my gear to overlook the lake. Early April in the Yukon means that the peak itself was still covered with snow but I'd packed for that, though the final couple of kilometers had been tougher than I had expected. Still, being out and about at least cleared my mind of the dismal state of my life after moving to Whitehorse. No job, barely enough money to pay next month's rent and having just broken up with my girlfriend, leaving on a Tuesday on my junker of a car was just what the doctor ordered. As bad as my life had been, I'm pretty sure I wasn't even close to breaking down, at least not enough to see things.

I shut my eyes, forcing them to stay shut for a count of three before I open them again. The blue box stays, taunting me with its reality. I can feel my breathing shorten, my thoughts splitting in a thousand different directions as I try to make sense of what's happening.

Stop.

I force my eyes close again and old training, old habits come into play. I bottle up the feelings of panic that encroach on my mind, force my scattered thoughts to stop swirling and compartmentalise my feelings. This is not the time or place for all this. I shove it all into a box and close the lid, pushing my emotions down until all there is a comforting, familiar, numbness.

A therapist once said my emotional detachment is a learned self-defence mechanism, one that was useful during my youth but somewhat unnecessary now that I'm an adult with more control over my surroundings. My girlfriend, my ex-girlfriend, just called me an emotionless dick. I've been taught better coping mechanisms but when push comes to shove, I go with what works. If there's an environment which I can't control, I'm going to call floating blue boxes in the real world one of them.

Calmer now, I open my eyes and re-read the information. First rule – what is, is. No more arguing or screaming or worrying about why or how or if I'm insane. What is, is. So. I have perks. And there's a system providing the perks and assigning levels. There's also going to be dungeons and monsters. I'm in a frigging MMO without a damn manual it looks like, which means that at least some of my misspent youth is going to be useful. I wonder what my dad would say. I push the familiar flash of anger down at the thought of him, focusing instead on my current problems.

My first requirement is information. Or better yet, a guide. I'm working on instinct here, going by what feels right rather than what I think is right since the thinking part of me is busy putting its fingers in its ears and going 'na-na-na-na-na'.

"Status?" I query and a new screen blooms.

Status Screen			
Name	John Lee	Class	None
Race	Human (Male)	Level	0
Titles			
None			
Health	100	Stamina	100
Mana	100		
Status			
Twisted ankle (-5% movement speed) Tendinitis (-10% Manual Agility)			
Attributes			
Strength	11	Agility	10
Constitution	11	Perception	14
Intelligence	16	Willpower	18
Charisma	8	Luck	7
Skills			
None			
Class Skills			
None			
Spells			
None			

Unassigned Attributes:
1 Small, 1 Medium, 1 Large, 1 Greater Perk
Would you like to assign these attributes? (Y/N)

The second window pop's up almost immediately on top of the first. I want more time to look over my Status but the information seems mostly self-explanatory and it's better to get this over with. It's not as if I have a lot of time. Almost as soon as I think that, the Y depresses and a giant list of Perks flashes up.

Oh, I do **not** have time for this. I definitely don't have time to get stuck in character creation. Being stuck in a zone that is way out of my Level when the System initializes is a one-way ticket to chowville. The giant list of perks before me is way too much to even begin sorting through, especially with names that don't necessarily make sense. What the hell does Adaptive Coloring actually mean? Right, this system seems to work via thought, reacting to what I think so, perhaps I can sort by perk type – narrow it down to small perks for a guide or companion of some form?

Almost as soon as I think of it, the system flashes out and only the word Companion appears. I nod slightly to myself and further details appear, providing two options.

AI   *Spirit*

I select AI but a new notice flashes up

AI Selection unavailable. *Minimum requirements of:*
Mark IV Processing Unit not met

I grunt. Yeah, no shit. I don't have a computer on me. Or... in me? No cyberpunk world for me. Not yet at least, though how cool would that be with a computer for a brain and metallic arms that don't hurt from being on the computer too much. Not the time for this, so I pick Spirit next and I acknowledge the query.

System Companion Spirit gained
Congratulations! World Fourth. As the fourth individual to gain a Companion Spirit, your companion is now (Linked). Linked Companions will grow and develop with you.

As I dismiss the notifications, I can see a light begin to glow to my right. I twist around, wondering who or what my new companion is going to be.

"Run, hide or fight. Ain't hard to make a choice boy-o."

Look, I'm no pervert. I didn't need a cute, beautiful fairy as my System Companion Spirit. Sure, a part of me hoped for it, I'm a red-blooded male who wouldn't mind staring at something pretty. Still, practically speaking, I would have settled for a Genderless automaton that was efficient and answered my questions with a minimum of lip. Instead, I get… him.

I stare at my new Companion and sigh mentally. Barely a foot tall, he's built like a linebacker with a full, curly brown beard. Brown hair, brown eyes and olive skin in a body-hugging orange jumpsuit that's tight in all the wrong places completes the ensemble. Ali my new companion has been here for all of 10 minutes giving me the lowdown and I'm already partly regretting my choice.

Partly, because for all of his berating, he's actually quite useful.

"Run," I finally decide, pulling apart the chocolate bar and taking another bite. No use fighting, nothing in the store that could scratch a Level 110 monster is going to be usable by me according to Ali and while there's no guarantee one of them will spawn immediately, even the lower level monsters that will make up its dinner would be too tough for me.

Hiding just delays things, so I have to get the hell out of the park which really, shouldn't be that hard. It took me half-a-day of hard hiking to get up this far in the mountain from the parking lot and the parking lot is just inside the new zone. At a good pace, I should be down in a few hours which if I understand things properly means there aren't that many monsters. Once I'm out, it seems

Whitehorse has a Safe Zone, which means I can hunker down and figure out what the hell is going on.

"About damn time," grouses Ali. A wave of his hands and a series of new windows appear in front of me. Shortly after appearing he demanded full access to my System which has allowed him to manipulate the information I can see and receive. It's going a lot faster this way since he just pushes the information to me, letting me read through things while he does the deeper search. The new blue windows - System messages according to him - are his picks for medium and large perks respectively.

Prodigy: Subterfuge

You're a natural born spy. Intrepid would hire you immediately.

Effect: All Subterfuge skills are gained 100% quicker. +50% Skill Level increase for all Subterfuge skills.

"Why this?" I frown, poking at the Subterfuge side. I'm not exactly the spying kind, more direct in most of my interactions. I've never really felt the need to lie too much and I certainly don't see myself creeping around breaking into buildings.

"Stealth skills. It gives a direct bonus to all of them which means you'll gain them faster. A small perk would allow us to directly affect the base

Stealth skill but at this level, we've got to go up to its main category." Ali replies and continues, "If you manage to survive, it'll probably be useful in the future anyway."

Quantum Stealth Manipulator (QSM)

The QSM allows its bearer to phase-shift, placing himself adjacent to the current dimension

Effect: While active, user is rendered invisible and undetectable to normal and magical means as long as the QSM is active. Solid objects may be passed through but will drain charge at a higher rate. Charge lasts 5 minutes under normal conditions.

"The QSM – how do I recharge it?"

"It uses a Type III Crystal Manipulator. The Crystal draws upon ambient and line specific..." Ali stares at my face for a moment before waving his hand. "It recharges automatically. It'll be fully charged in a day under normal conditions."

"No Level requirements on these?"

"None."

I picked Ali because he knows the System better than I do, so I can either accept what he's saying or I can do it myself. Put that way, there's really not much of a choice. It's what we talked about, though that Perk Subterfuge isn't really going to be that useful for me. On the other hand, any bonuses to staying out of sight would be great and the QSM would let me run away if I was found out. Which just left my Greater Perk.

Advanced Class: Erethran Honor Guard

The Erethran Honor Guard are Elite Members of the Erethran Armed Forces.

Class Abilities: +2 Per Level in Strength. + 4 Per Level in Constitution and Agility. +3 Per Level in Intelligence and Willpower. Additional 3 Free Attributes per Level.

+90% Mental Resistance. +40% Elemental Resistance

May designate a Personal Weapon. Personal Weapon is Soulbound and upgradeable.

Honor Guard members may have up to 4 Hard Point Links before Essence Penalties apply.

Warning! Minimum Attribute Requirements for the Erethran Honor Guard Class not met. Class Skills Locked till minimum requirements met.

Advanced Class: Dragon Knight

Groomed before birth, Dragon Knights are the Elite Warriors of the Kingdom of Xylargh.

Class Abilities: +3 Per Level in Strength and Agility. + 4 Per Level in Constitution. +3 Per Level Intelligence and Willpower. + 1 in Charisma. Additional 2 Free Attributes per Level.

+80% Mental Resistance. +50% Elemental Resistance

Gain One Greater and One Lesser Elemental Affinity

Warning! Minimum Attribute Requirements for the Dragon Knight Class not met. Class Skills Locked till minimum requirements met.

"That's it?"

"No, you could get this too."

Class: Demi-God

You sexy looking human, you'll be a demi-god. Smart, strong, handsome. What more could you want?
Class Abilities: +100 to all Attributes
All Greater Affinities Gained
Super Sexiness Trait

"That's not a thing."

"It really ain't," smirking, Ali waves and the last screen dismisses. "You wanted a class that helps you survive? That means mental resistances. Otherwise, you'll be pissing those pretty little Pac-Man boxers the moment you see a Level 50 monster. You wanted an end-game? The Honor Guard are some mean motherfuckers. They combine magic and tech making them one of the most versatile groups around, and their Master class advancements are truly scary. The Dragon Knights fight Dragons. One on one and they sometimes even win. Oh, and neither, and I quote 'makes me into a monster'.

"If these are Advanced Classes, what other classes are there?" I prod at Ali, still hesitating. This seems like a big choice.

"Basic, Advance, Master, Grandmaster, Heroic, Legendary," lists Ali and he shrugs. "I could get you a Master Class with your perk, but you'd be locked out of your Class Skills forever. You'd also take forever to level because of the higher minimum experience level gains. Instead, I've got you a rare Advanced Class - it'll give you a better base stat gain per level and you won't have to wait forever to gain access to your Class Skills. Getting a Basic Class, even a rarer Basic Class would be a waste of the Greater Perk. So, what's it going to be?"

As cool as punching a dragon in the face would be, I know which way I'm going the moment he called it up. I mentally select the Guard and light fills me. At first, it just forces me to squint but it begins to dig in, pushing into my body and mind, sending electric, hot claws into my cells. The pain is worse than anything I've felt and I've broken bones, shattered ribs and even managed to electrocute myself before. I know I'm screaming but the pain keeps coming, swarming over me and tearing at my mind, my control. Luckily, darkness claims me before my mind shatters.

Read Life in the North now:
https://readerlinks.com/l/976138